THE
WATCHMAN'S
RAINBOW

AND OTHER WORKS

BILL WYANT

The Watchman's Rainbow and Other Works

2019 © William Wyant

ISBN: 978-0-9600201-0-2

William Dexter Wyant
williamwyant@comcast.net

CONTENTS

DEDICATION

On our fiftieth wedding anniversary, Norma and I were given a framed photograph of our immediate family: We, our children, their spouses and our grandchildren. I thought they were the best measure of the worth of my life. It is to them that I dedicate this work.

PRELUDE TO A DREAM

In the beginning, a work is not a work at all.
It is first an idea, perhaps only a dream.
Then it is a plan with all its pieces in place.
Then it is pieces scattered about like a dream shattered.
That is a hard time.
The pieces may drift away as if on a tide at ebb;
The dream may fade as day gives way to night.
Then pieces come together, dream becomes reality.
But soon we are dreaming again,
and planning again with all the pieces in place,
and staring again at pieces scattered about like a dream
    shattered;
and that is a hard time.

Life can be a crowded freeway or a country lane, with forks and roundabouts and paths hidden almost to the instant we might pass them by. We can limit our journey to a single way or wander aimlessly, and we'll likely do a bit of both. But, as J. R. R. Tolkien tells us, "Not all who wander are lost."

    Writing an essay or a play or a poem or a story is an act designed to produce a work. The quality of the work is for others to say, but the decision to work is ours alone.

THE WATCHMAN'S RAINBOW

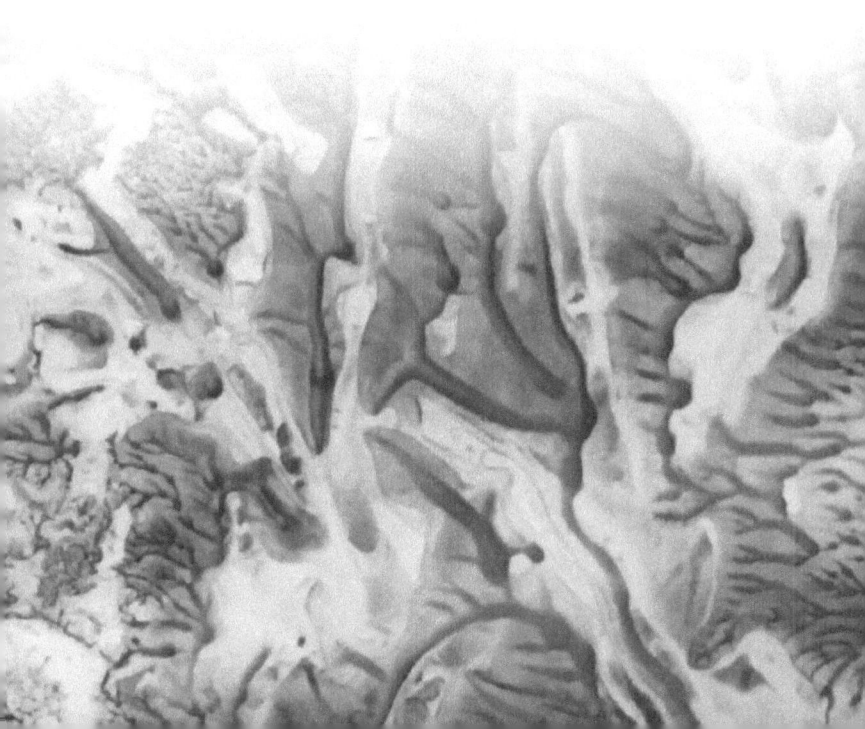

AUTHOR'S NOTE

THE CHARACTERS IN THE STORY that follows are fictitious. But for the characters themselves, the lives and events in which they are portrayed are real. As if in another universe, they lived the events related by their equally fictitious narrator.

The model for this approach is real: Arthur Conan Doyle, whose fictitious consulting detective, Sherlock Holmes, was chronicled by equally fictitious Doctor Watson. Holmes's reality is exemplified in three nonfiction books written after his final fictitious adventure. *Sherlock's Logic* (1985) is a nonfiction book in which the author, William Neblett, " . . . draws the reader into the world of logical deduction by way of . . . a unique and entertaining illustration of the various forms of reasoning, correct and fallacious, deductive and inductive, and a demonstration of how logic is present in everyday life." Daniel Smith gave us *How to Think Like Sherlock* (2012) so we might "learn Holmes's method . . . his system for sorting clues from trivia, truth from lies, and guilt from innocence." And in *The Science of Sherlock Holmes* (2016), E. J. Wagner quotes one of the preeminent forensic scientists of the early

20th century as suggesting "that students of forensic science read the Sherlock Holmes tales as examples of proper scientific approach and to obtain a perspective on the new directions forensic science might take." In her final two sentences, Wagner offers an appropriate caveat, "He (Doyle) wrote of science but viewed through a storyteller's lens. Even Conan Doyle sometimes saw but did not observe."

Thus, the fictitious character may be brought to life through nonfiction prose.

In the story below, we enter a corner of the mind of our narrator, Simon Stoddard, Esq. The corner is populated by characters who engage in activities that are quite real. Pick up any nonfiction book about the Cold War, read and listen to the news of any day, wonder about the boundary between historic fiction and narrative history, perhaps wander along a darkly lit corridor in your own mind.

The central character's life is defined by two arcs presented in different narrative styles to illuminate the opportunity costs associated with life's irrevocable choices. The principal characters exhibit personal arcs—from pasts relative to presents when arcs intersect those of others to the future, subsequent presents, and to remind us that like life, "It ain't over 'til it's over."

PROLOGUE

Every man has his secret sorrows
which the world knows not;
and often times we call a man cold
when he is only sad.
—Henry Wadsworth Longfellow

LAWYERS ARE SUPPOSED to be able to discern facts, to separate wheat from chaff. But a good story often falls
short of the rules of evidence and due process. Creative
nonfiction some call it. I have files and confidences, of
course, and transcriptions of surveillance recordings
obtained from sources that must remain nameless.
From time to time while telling the story I lapse into
historical fiction, remaining true to the spirit of events
but fashioning dialogue and filling in gaps based upon
my knowledge of people and events. Actual names and
places, as you might expect, are hidden in the shadows,
and the passage of time and human memory may have
had some impact on the narration.

As the Cold War wound down, the world was awash
with restless warriors experienced in arts and crafts
no longer thought necessary to international relations

among peace-loving nations. Some found their careers cut short and their fortunes bleak, but some having exceptional resumes found bountiful opportunities in a growing market for private security and paramilitary forces, industrial intelligence and same ol', same ol'. This is a story of one such man.

Like most stories, it begins before the beginning and ends after the final bell has rung. But, as a narrative must commence somewhere . . .

I

Special Report to the *Mid-Country Clarion*

4 Killed, 2 Wounded in Downtown Shootout
This morning at the corner of Main and 4th Streets, four men died and two, including Police Chief Devon Xander, were wounded as a fusillade of bullets from automatic weapons ricocheted off buildings and pavement. Dead were Reuben Ulrich, night auditor at the Marcus Hotel on Main Street, and three men yet to be identified. Chief Xander and Patrolman Timothy Murphy were wounded in the exchange of gunfire between the police and the three unidentified assailants and were later treated and released from City Hospital.

AVERAGE HEIGHT AND WEIGHT, nondescript, someone you'd pass by but hardly notice. Oh, you'd avoid the space occupied by the mass, but nothing to call to mind. Whether wearing a raincoat in the rain, topcoat on a frosty morning, or a midnight blue suit at a formal reception, everything merged into the time and the place and the situation.

Amos Sanson entered this universe through the jungles and mountains of Southeast Asia and Latin America where stealth and observation enabled him to locate enemy threats to his comrades and employers. From there, his skills were practiced in hunting grounds throughout the world. He became a calm and capable sensing platform, observing whats and wheres, and whens and whos and hows . . . the whys belonging to someone else; the present only . . . the past and future belonging to someone else.

The business district was three square blocks of specialty shops and professionals' offices, with a sprinkling of colorful restaurants for icing. It was a small city, comfortable for the residents but perhaps a bit less so for strangers. From his perch in a corner room on the second floor over a bookstore on the corner of 4th and Main, Sanson could see everything that moved on the streets, from the hotel around the corner to the bank.

Among the things he noticed right away was an office across the street from the bookstore. When the venetian blinds were open, Sanson often saw the neatly uniformed police chief watching. Bay windows extended from the two outer walls of his corner office, affording clear views each way along the intersecting streets.

From the hotel on Main Street, Sanson's target, Reuben Ulrich, walked daily around the corner, past the police station, to deposit the day's cash receipts in the downtown branch of a local bank. Ulrich was afraid and vulnerable. He had betrayed people who brutally punished disloyalty. He appeared to be unaware of the surveillance team following him in a smooth, well-orchestrated ABC operation.

Sanson video-recorded his observations and uploaded the information to a computer address that changed with every transmission. He wondered whether the man in the bay window had noticed the ABC surveillance of his subject, and if he did, what he might do about it.

Ulrich stepped out of the bank and turned right toward the police station and the intersection of 4th and Main. ABC moved with him, two following and one across the street. When Ulrich reached the street corner, ABC walked rapidly toward him, drawing submachine guns from under their coats and loosing well-aimed shots, dropping him into a widening pool of his own blood.

Chief Devon Xander and Patrolman Tim Murphy ran out of the police station with guns drawn and turned toward the intersection. Quickly assessing the situation, Xander and Murphy fired at the three gunmen. Two of them were struck down immediately, but the third staggered both officers with short bursts.

With sirens wailing, police cruisers converged on the intersection, slid sideways and stopped to block the roadways. Patrolmen leapt from their cars and fired at the standing gunman. He spun and joined his companions face down on the sidewalk. The ABC team, expecting to escape before the small-city police could react, had underestimated the force prepared for rapid response and professional action by Chief Xander.

As quickly as it had begun, it was over. Reuben Ulrich lay on the sidewalk with the three gunmen. The chief and his deputy shakily approached the intersection, holding free hands against bleeding wounds. The other officers formed a protective shield around the crime scene and looked to the wounds of Xander and Murphy.

Amos Sanson had recorded the attack and encounter between ABC and the police. He uploaded the information, and after a short pause received a reply, "Leave now!" Immediately, leaving the observation equipment and computer behind, Sanson went down the back stairs and disappeared into the maze of small shops and seedy hotels bordering the city center.

Later, in a small hotel outside the police cordon, Sanson watched the newscasts and read the local newspaper accounts. They showed nothing beyond the bare events of the day, but the reporters did not hesitate to pose questions and suggest answers. A difference between Sanson and the press: Sanson did not question.

But somewhere, someone who did care about the answers to many questions that did not matter to Sanson smiled and raised his glass to his associates.

Three days later, Chief Xander walked into the café at the intercity bus depot, his left arm in a sling, noting that a neatly dressed middle-aged man was sitting alone on a counter stool near the entrance to the passenger loading platform, cradling a cup of coffee in both hands, gazing into the mirror behind the counter as if deep in thought. On the stool beside him were a neatly folded, well-worn raincoat and hat, and between the two stools rested an equally well-worn suitcase.

Xander sat down on the stool next to the hat and coat, ordered a cup of coffee, and glancing obliquely into the mirror behind the counter, noticed that, though the dark early morning was warm and humid, the man was wearing soft cloth gloves matched to the coat and hat.

"Good morning," Xander said, glancing at the man's reflection in the mirror. "Warm day coming."

Amos Sanson, continuing his thoughtful gaze, nodded.

"I see you are wearing gloves," the Chief continued. "Mind telling me why?"

Sanson, still looking into the mirror, slowly raised his right hand and began, with his left hand, to carefully remove his right glove, revealing the red, tautly drawn skin of a deformed hand. Xander nodded. Sanson slowly returned his hand to the comfort and protection of the glove.

Just then, the loud speaker behind the counter blared, "The west-bound express bus is now ready for boarding and will depart in five minutes."

Slowly, Amos Sanson rose from his seat, laid a five-dollar bill alongside his coffee cup, collected his hat and coat, picked up the suitcase with his left hand, and with a brief nod toward the police chief walked through the door onto the passenger platform. A few minutes later, Chief Xander heard gears grind and saw a bus back out of the angled parking lane of the '50s-era bus terminal and drive away. In a moment, it was gone.

Devon Xander sipped his coffee and thought about the neatly dressed man with the raincoat, hat, and suitcase . . . and the damaged right hand. Curious? The man was a stranger and was departing in the wee hours of the morning a few days after the unexplained violent deaths of four men. The chief filed the thoughts in an appropriate drawer in his mind and returned to his coffee.

As the bus pulled away from the city, Sanson reviewed the encounter with the policeman. He knew he had revealed much, and he knew that the chief had ways to satisfy his professional curiosities. Perhaps it was time for this leopard to change his spots.

In the early-morning quiet, Chief Xander sat at his desk in the police station, unlocked the file in his mind, and extracted the information about the brief encounter at the bus station diner. He had little to go on, but his curiosity was aroused. As he sat in the predawn quiet, images of the events of the last few days and this morning slowly merged.

He had a good look at the man at the bus station. The routine investigation of the area surrounding the deadly attack had revealed the temporary occupancy of a room over the bookstore that provided a clear view of the crime scene from the bank on 4th Street to the Marcus Hotel on Main. The owner of the building had given him a partial description of a man seen entering and leaving the door to the back stairs leading up to the room. The owner, who was also the proprietor of the bookstore on the ground floor, was an old friend with whom Xander often talked about books, local politics, and world events. Xander had a high regard for her knowledge and analytical acumen. Her scant description fit many middle-aged men, including the quiet man with whom he had shared the diner earlier. Especially noted in her description, however, was a cloth glove that matched his raincoat but seemed out of place in the warmth of the recent weather.

Xander concluded that connections might exist.

Rosada Ángel Jesús had come to State College as its principal reference librarian. She had retired from federal service after a career that began in Washington, DC, took her to posts throughout Latin America, and brought her back to DC. At the college she immediately established herself as a scholarly librarian whose skills enriched the institution's research and learning environment. The faculty loved working with her, and students thought of her as a doting aunt constantly uplifting their academic interests. When the owner of the bookstore at 4th and Main retired, Rosada bought the store and the building that housed it. She reveled in her new role as bookseller. Now, she was "reference librarian" to the neighborhood as well as the college.

Chief Xander was immediately drawn to the ebullient proprietor and spent time almost every day in conversation at the coffee bar in the store's corner windows. From there, he could watch the streets, and ask questions endlessly. Rosada loved having the inquisitive policeman in her shop and found many of Xander's questions stimulating in a way she remembered from her earlier career.

Settling into a cozy chair, Rosada placed her herbal tea on a low table piled high with books, looked across the table at Xander, and, in a reminiscing tone, continued her response to one of his endless questions, "After the breakup of the Soviet Union, intelligence, military, and law enforcement professionals no longer needed to fight the Cold War roamed the world, selling their services to industry, governments, politicians and non-governmental organizations. Generally, they're available to all who can pay. It's big business, operating for high stakes."

Xander understood. During his Army military police deployments to the Balkans and Afghanistan, he had encountered many experienced operatives who fit Rosada's narration.

From the questions asked by Chief Xander's investigators, Rosada had inferred that the man upstairs was a "person of interest" in the recent killings. After talking with Xander and learning more about the execution of the assassination, she suspected that it was not a typical small-city mystery. Although the failure to appreciate the unusual quality of Xander's police force had caught the hit team off guard, the team's techniques reminded her of some she had analyzed in her former life.

With a slight lowering of her eyes, Rosada smiled to herself, an absent-minded behavior that Xander noticed. Curiously, some seemingly unrelated dots were connecting in his mind.

A month passed without adding to Xander's information about the incident. His inquiries through regular law-enforcement channels had provided nothing of substance, and though the crime weighed heavily upon his mind, eventually other matters caught him up in police routine. His moments in Rosada's shop were fleeting, and she was constantly involved in her dual roles. For both, days were long on the minutiae of their respective businesses. At that very moment, Rosada was attending a book fair in Indianapolis.

Rosada approached the refreshments table in the lobby of the convention center. She had just ambled through the reference and nonfiction rooms, pausing here and there to leaf through a volume or exchange conversation and business cards with a publisher's representative. As she filled her teacup with hot water, she noticed a man dressed neatly in a business suit, holding a coffee cup in his left hand and cradling a book in the crook of his right arm. As he turned slightly to his right, she noticed something that nearly evoked a gasp: a cloth-gloved right hand. She watched him move easily and quietly across the room toward a cluster of comfortable chairs in a well-lit corner. Quietly, Rosada aimed the camera in her cell phone and clicked several snapshots. Moving away from the corner, she dialed Xander's cell phone and sent him the pictures with a brief question, "Look familiar?" Immediately appeared a response, "Yes."

Rosada eased herself into a chair in the corner cluster, busied herself with her tea and a few brochures, and glanced at the man sitting nearby. She sighed and said, "Well, it seems to be the usual problem of separating the wheat from the chaff . . . lots of books, but who knows which ones are most likely to sell." "Yes, the bookseller's conundrum," came the quiet reply. Offering her right hand, she introduced herself. "Hi. I'm Rosada Jesús." Raising his eyes from the open book in his lap and setting aside his coffee cup, he softly grasped her hand and responded, "Amos Sanson."

Sanson did not recognize Rosada. He had not met the owner of the building at 4th and Main. All arrangements had been made without his involvement; he had only to go there, complete his mission, and walk away.

Rosada offered her business card to Sanson, and he handed her his. Quickly scanning her card, he was startled by her business address. He checked his meeting agenda and his watch, then asked Rosada if she would accompany him to the book fair's closing luncheon. Chatting about books they had noted while touring the publishers' displays, they walked toward the dining room. After a pleasant lunch, Sanson and Rosada shook hands and said good-bye.

After receiving Amos Sanson's photographs and business address from Rosada, Xander called some of his contacts and discovered that Sanson was a respectable businessman and Army veteran. The disquieting factor, however, was the lack of detail about his past . . . he seemed to have emerged from nowhere into a life made to order. Skirting regular channels, Xander called two old friends who had been part of his mobile training teams in the Balkans and Afghanistan and now were federal investigators. Both reported rumors of a reconnaissance/surveillance expert, meeting the description of Xander's person of interest, who had disappeared in the mountains of Colombia or Panama while working for US Drug Enforcement advisors. At the same time, Rosada had contacted a former coworker who recalled hearing of a DEA tracker/surveillance contractor who had been held briefly by a drug cartel somewhere in the Central America / South America border region, was treated "roughly" and escaped, and was administratively retired because he was believed to be irreparably damaged physically and psychologically. While neither of these inquiries turned up information meeting the standards of legal proof, both were plausible reports from reliable sources.

Shortly after his inquiries, Xander received a message in a familiar format, "Man meeting your description seen several times recently on second-floor balcony of the Meridor Café in Panama City's Casco Viejo from sunset minus 15 to plus 45. Suggest you take a look."

In a small city several miles away from the book fair, Amos Sanson inserted a key into a dead-bolt lock, turned the key, opened the door, and entered a small, neatly arrayed second-floor apartment over a modest, national-chain bookstore. For the second time in recent weeks, Sanson felt threatened. He knew that the results accompanying many of his assignments crossed the line, and while previously he had neither known nor cared about the ultimate outcomes, he was beginning to think about the consequences of his actions. He knew Xander to be an able policeman; and, from the small talk with Rosada, he suspected that she might be able to see into the shadows that cloaked his activities. Meanwhile, another mission was in motion, a mission that might provide a point of departure into a new life.

In the predawn darkness, Sanson was awakened by soft beeps from his secure satellite phone. He read as the text filled the screen: "It's on. Be in country within two days. Xander is on his way and remains unaware of your plan." Satisfied, Sanson acknowledged the message and went back to sleep.

From a doorway across the street, Sanson watched Devon Xander enter the Meridor Café. A moment later, Xander appeared at a balcony table, sitting where he could see the entrance into the second-floor bar and watch the sun descend into the western sea. Fifteen minutes before sunset, Sanson crossed the street, entered the bar, and much to Xander's surprise, walked directly toward him, stopped at his table, and with a brief bow said quietly, "Buenos tardes, Señor Xander. May I join you?"

Xander pointed to the chair opposite him. Sanson sat, and the waiter brought him a light red wine of local vintage.

For a few moments, they sipped their drinks. Then Sanson broke the silence.

"You are quite persistent."

"Perhaps even lucky."

"Luck can be helpful, but by far, the greater gifts are experience and preparation. Please permit me to explain why you have been brought here."

"Brought here?"

"For my current project, I require a reliable partner. You are experienced and know the value of preparation. And, I believe you can be trusted."

"Compliments, but nothing of substance."

"A few weeks ago, rebels kidnapped a senior executive of Seaboard Shipping. They are holding him at a remote ranch in the mountains. They hope to convince Seaboard to assist their enterprise. Failing that, they will simply negotiate a considerable ransom. Seaboard is negotiating. Their risk assessment, however, favors a rescue attempt. I am to spot their rescue operation, and for that I need a reliable partner to protect me while I concentrate on bringing the rescue team onto the target."

Before dusk, Sanson reported that he was in position to guide the rescue team to the shed where the hostage was being held. He had not informed mission control that Xander was with him. Xander was his security blanket.

Shortly after dark, Sanson's earphone commanded, "Paint the target." He pushed a button just as two unmarked helicopters descended silently into the clearing in front of the sheds and the main house. One chopper moved toward one of the sheds and three shadowy figures stepped onto the ground, moved directly to the shed, broke open the door, threw a package into the shed, and returned to the hovering aircraft. As the helicopter lifted into the air, the shed exploded in flames and flying debris. Suddenly, the clearing was bathed in light and armed men were running out of the main house. The second helicopter opened fire, dropping several of the men and shredding the front of the house, and followed the first out of the clearing.

A message sounded in Sanson's ear, "Pickup at LZ Alpha Mike, Out."

Sanson was already moving. He piled the surveillance and targeting equipment upon a thermite grenade and pulled the pin. Followed closely by Xander, he moved quickly along their planned escape route. But, he was not going to LZ Alpha Mike.

"We're on our own."

"What happened back there?"

"Later."

Grabbing Sanson's arm, Xander stopped and turned him. "Now!"

Xander felt the point of Sanson's knife against his throat. "Now is not the time. We must move quickly! I was briefed for a *rescue* mission."

Xander loosed his grip on Sanson's arm. With Sanson leading, they hurried along the path.

Two days later, at 11 a.m., at his regular table on the balcony of the Meridor, Sanson sat reading the news about a jungle shootout between two drug cartels. Killed in the crossfire was a shipping official being held for ransom by one of the cartels.

Xander crossed the room and sat down. Immediately, the waiter placed two cups of steaming coffee on the table. "Is now a good time?" Sanson handed him the paper. "Now is a very good time."

Sanson concluded his explanation, paused briefly, and continued, "The lines have become blurred. No longer am I comfortable with the old ways. On this card is the name of my attorney. I would like to instruct him that he may meet with you as my partner. We will ask Ms. Jesús to support our activities with her impeccable research and analysis. If you agree to the arrangement we have discussed, join me for breakfast here between 1000 and noon tomorrow. If not, simply board your plane tomorrow afternoon and fly home."

The following morning, Sanson finished his breakfast and signaled for coffee. It was 1155. He looked out at the sun-swept, undulating sea. At the sound of foot-steps, he turned expecting to see the waiter with his coffee. Xander nodded. Gesturing to the waiter, Sanson smiled and said, "Dos tazas de café, por favor."

Rosada Jesús sat comfortably in her bookstore coffee corner listening intently as Xander reported. Xander paused for a moment, then concluded, "During a lay-over in my flight home, I was engaged in conversation by an impeccably dressed fellow traveler. He handed me this." Rosada removed a folded paper from the envelope Xander gave her and read:

> Reports originating in Colombia indicate that a senior Seaboard Shipping executive believed to have died in the crossfire between warring drug cartels was really the victim of a well-orchestrated assassination directed by unknown forces. The death of Armando Garcia, Seaboard's chief operating officer, had been defined as collateral damage resulting from a battle for dominance in the lucrative narcotics trade. The reports also described the farmstead "shed" in which Garcia died as a modestly luxurious bungalow at a safe house maintained by the public prosecutor.

Rosada felt herself easing back into a world she thought she'd put behind her. Initially adversaries, Sanson and Xander had collaborated to capitalize on their professional skills and ensure their survival. She had seen such transformations before and was not surprised by twists and turns leading to an unexpected outcome and a shared sense of betrayal.

For now, however, Xander had reappeared after a brief immersion in a sea of contradictions, and Sanson had disappeared into the shadows that had harbored him for so long.

II

THE ROAD NOT TAKEN

YANKEE'S: SUBDUED AND QUIET, simply named and adorned with photographs and baseball memorabilia—Joe DiMaggio, Phil Rizzuto, Yogi Berra and many others, all in New York Yankee pinstripes—patronized by friend and foe alike in the small town in Appalachia defined by the crossing of two highways that carved the town into four quadrants. Catty-corner was the Palace Theater, and on the other two corners were the banks that gave prominence to this rural crossroads community of five or so thousands. On Saturday mornings, farmers and townsmen gathered on the four corners to argue politics, trade pocketknives and admire railroad watches while their wives attended to the business of their homes in the surrounding shops. Sooner or later, many of them wandered into Yankee's.

On a late August evening, six lifelong friends gathered for the first time since their high school graduation three months earlier. They had been "regulars" in Yankee's since childhood, having been introduced to the pub by their parents, themselves "regulars" and friends of the chief of the house, Joseph "Yankee" Timberlake, who ruled the front of the house while his wife commanded the kitchen. Yankee called them simply "The Six." They had not been together since graduating in May, and they were about to separate again. Mandy (Amanda Kay Armiston) and Brad (Arthur Bradley Cole), Suzanne (Sandra Suzanne Simington) and Wil (William Denton Broadmater III), Jan (Janet Sterling Trent) and John Paul (John Paul Anderson), sitting together at a round table under the watchful eyes of Yankee as he stood behind the bar and listened:

John Paul: We haven't been together since the night we graduated. We had great plans: where we're going, how we're going to get there. Well, summer's over and the real world awaits.

Mandy: And we're ready to go, aren't we Brad?

Brad: You bet!

Suzanne: Go where, Brad? Any changes since the *good old* high school days?

Brad: Yes! I thought then that I'd be headed for seminary this fall. But Monday I'm off to see the world, US Army style: basic training, medical corpsman school, and, well . . . you know how that goes.

Mandy: And I'm going to nursing school at Sacred Hearts. This summer Brad and I earned our EMT certificates. We even delivered a baby on our last run.

Wil: That's quite a change since May, Brad. What did your folks think about you going into the Army? That isn't exactly what I thought they had in mind.

Brad: They weren't real pleased; but, when I explained that I'm going to be a medical specialist and then go to PA school on the GI Bill, they came around. Even though he was a conscientious objector, Dad served as an ambulance driver in Spain and France in the '30s. When I get out of the Army, Mandy will be an RN and I'm going to PA school.

Wil: It sounds like you two are ready for what's coming. Suzanne and I are still going to State Teachers College. And I still want to coach the old green and gray with Coach Murphy.

Suzanne: All through high school we planned to be teachers, and nothing's changed. Hopefully, we can come back here to teach after we graduate.

Jan, wistfully: Coming home.

Suzanne: Wouldn't that be great! What about you, Jan? Still want to be a politician like your dad?

Jan: I don't think so. I really didn't like some of the stuff I saw in Dad's office this summer. Don't get me wrong; he's a great guy and a good state senator. But sometimes he went against the grain because someone wanted something special. Someday, I'd like to have the power, but use it to help folks who have a tough time getting along in this world. Things are getting pretty complicated out there . . . maybe I'll be able to smooth out the road for some who can't do so well on their own. So, it's business school, MBA, law school. Who knows, I might finish college in time to work long enough to earn Social Security.

Laughter came easily to The Six.

Brad: It's not like you to be so quiet, John Paul. Have you figured out where you're headed?

John Paul: Well, things are a bit up in the air. I'm going to keep my job with the contractor working on the highway bypass for a while . . . sort of hold the fort while you guys ride off at dawn.

Jan: You can make sure Yankee holds our table for us.

John Paul rose and raised his glass.

John Paul: Before we part, a toast.

John Paul turned and gestured toward Yankee, who was leaning on the bar, smiling.

John Paul: Listen close, Yankee! You're the witness to this solemn pledge.

Turning his gaze to the five seated at the table, John Paul continued: Brave companions, stand, raise your glasses and say with me.

They stood, raised their glasses, and spoke in solemn unison: We each do bid adieu, and pledge, each to all, all as one, to gather here on Friday night before each class reunion to tell not less than all the truths, nor more, and renew abiding love.

Then The Six looked at each other, drank, placed their glasses on the table, turned to face Yankee, and again in unison: Yo Yankee; Go Red Sox!

Laughing, they rushed through the front door as Yankee scowled and threw the bar towel at them, shouting: Flee, you . . . insufferables!

As he recovered the towel, Yankee muttered to himself: God keep you safe and happy.

Friday before their fifth-year high school reunion, five of the six (Brad and Mandy, Suzanne and Wil, and Jan) sat at their round table in Yankee's. Brad, his hand on Mandy's, looked on as each spoke, but he did not speak. He was there in spirit only.

Jan: It isn't like him to be late. Yankee, any word from John Paul?

Yankee: Not since the fall you all left. He worked for a while out on the bypass and then just sort of disappeared.

Jan: Well, it isn't like him to be late.

Suzanne: Jan, you know that he'd be here by now if he was coming. A theatrical late entrance would be just like him, but he wouldn't have waited this long.

Wil: Well, I'm dying to begin.

Suzanne: Then start, Coach.

Wil: OK. First, we renew the pledge. We haven't been together for a long time, and I think John Paul set the right agenda five years ago.

They stood and raised their glasses (all except Brad, of course): We pledge to join here on Friday night before each class reunion to tell not less than all the truths, nor more, and renew abiding love.

Wil: Yeah, it's pretty corny but it's our tradition and I'm sticking to it. The "adieu" part we'll save for later. When my knee and hip collapsed during that lacrosse game at the end of my sophomore year, I thought my life was over. But Suzanne sat me down one day and told me to quit mopping the floor with my chin. I had never been a quitter, and now wasn't the time to start, she said, and it is my motto today, "Don't you dare let what you can't do get in the way of what you can do." She continued, "You march right into Crafty's office and tell him you'll take the job of undergraduate assistant for the football scout team, and spend your time learning the playing styles of every opponent we face for the next two years." Crafty said that by the end of the next two years at State, I'd be a great high school coach. I did, and by golly I am. When Coach Murphy won the conference championship last year in football, guess who shared the sideline, and the limelight, with him. That's right . . . yours truly. The years at State paid off in spades. This season, it'll be official: assistant coach in football and lacrosse, and top dog in wrestling. I'm on track with a full head of steam. It doesn't get any better than that.

Suzanne: Not any better?

Wil: Well, now that you mention it, the picture might improve next June.

Suzanne: Might improve?

Jan: What's happening, as if I couldn't guess?

Suzanne: I think you guessed.

Mandy: Brad and I would have been there *this* June.

Suzanne: Yes.

For an instant, all were silent.

Jan: Well, I'll finish my MBA in August, and start law school in September. When our next reunion rolls around, I should be a member of the state bar. No, Yankee, not your bar.

Yankee: Thank God! It's tough enough dealing with the bunch of you on that side of the bar. Trying to work around you on this side would be a pain in the . . .

Jan: You should be so lucky! While I'm in law school, I'm going to shadow a corporate law professor my first year, and if all goes well, clerk for Judge Trent the summers after my second and third years.

Mandy: In January, I'll be the lead nurse in the trauma unit.

The others (except Brad, of course) speaking

together: That's great, Mandy. You certainly have made your mark.

Mandy, looking down at Brad's hand on hers, her words trailing off into silence: Brad would have finished his first year in PA school. He'd have been one of my orderlies this summer. Three more years and we'd have been . . .

Mandy, staring vacantly into a distant place: I miss him . . . a lot. His folks just can't get past it. They say that losing a child is really tough on parents; children are supposed to outlive their parents . . . so they say. We studied the grieving process in nursing school, and God knows I've seen my share of grief in the ER, but I don't seem to be able to help his mom deal with it. His dad took it real hard at first, but he understood. After serving in Spain, he hung around Paris, and when the Nazis invaded, he drove ambulances for the French. Then the Germans captured him, but when they found out he was American, they paroled him and he came back home to stay. He understood Brad's desire to save lives. They say "time heals all hurt"; I often wonder how much time . . .

For a moment no one spoke.

Wil, breaking the silence: It's time, now, for the "bid adieu" part. Brave companions, stand and raise your glasses, drink the salute to now and five years from now, and let's head back over to the dance. It's supposed to go on till the wee hours, and though I'm a bit gimpy, I can still swing.

Mandy: You guys go on ahead. I'll be along in a few minutes.

Suzanne: We'll wait too, Mandy; we'll all go together.

For a moment they sat in silence.

Mandy broke the silence, beginning pensively, but becoming increasingly bitter as she spoke: He hated the killing and dying, but he could not shake that god-awful sense of duty. He just kept going back, time after time, trying to save every one of those godforsaken boys in that goddamned place.

Tears streaming, Mandy continued: Until the last second of my life, I will despise every one of those stupid politicians who sent them there where he could not help but help.

The only sound was the tinkle of glass on glass as Yankee placed the one he had just dried on the shelf behind the bar.

Five years later, on Friday evening before their tenth-year reunion, five of the six (Brad and Mandy, Suzanne and Wil, and Jan) gathered at their regular table in Yankee's. Only three spoke; Brad and Mandy, hand in hand, looked on silently.

Jan: I guess he isn't coming.

Suzanne: Jan, you know he would be here if he could.

Jan: I know, but ten years without a word. You'd think someone would have heard something in all this time.

Suzanne: He always had that quiet side.

Wil: Well, we're here and we honor the pledge. Murphy retires next year; then I'm taking over football and lacrosse. With wrestling in the winter, I'll be coaching all year long. It's exciting, but a little scary.

Suzanne: You'll be great, Wil. It's what you've worked so hard for the last ten years. My teaching load will be reduced this year, just one section each of English and

Spanish, because I've accepted the appointment as assistant principal. My focus will be on national testing and curriculum development. And Wil and I will move into my homeplace before school begins; we've got our work cut out for us.

Jan: A block off Main Street and two blocks from the school. Things are really working for you guys. I'll be the managing partner in January. They tell me I'm ready to run the place, but I think they just want more time to play golf. But, it works for me, so I'm looking forward to it. I'll be able to schedule my cases and balance my work between consumer law and practice management. The downside is that I'll be up in the capital, so I won't have much time back home.

Suzanne: Anything more personal in your career plans?

Jan: I don't think I'll have much time for a personal life. Yankee, I think we're ready now.

Yankee: On the way.

They sat quietly as Yankee placed their drinks on the table. Then they raised their glasses and directed silent salutes to the three "empty" chairs.

Jan: I still can't get over Mandy.

Wil: She seemed to be OK. She was perfect in her job in the trauma unit, always calm and confident, never rattled no matter how crazy the people around her were. And she was great with our young athletes. They always think their lives are over because they can't play for a while, but she seemed to talk them back on track, or help them cope with the rehab, or if their playing days were ended, adjust and find other productive paths. She was as much counselor as she was healer.

Suzanne: Yes, but she never talked about him.

Jan: I thought when she married Jason that she had put the past behind her. I knew she could never forget Brad, but I thought she was getting on with her life.

Suzanne: Her work seemed to console her . . . then it became a constant reminder of pain and suffering. The marriage seemed right at the beginning, but as she drifted away from Jason, she drifted away from everyone. Looking back, it's easy to see her drifting toward that horrible decision. I missed it when it counted most, and it will haunt me forever.

Yankee: And she dropped in here more and more often. I've seen a lot of people come and go; I didn't see her go. You weren't the only one who missed it, Suzanne.

Wil: Maybe a busy year is the best thing for us. I don't know what lies ahead, but we are ready to take the field. So, drink up, ladies, and let's get started on the rest of our lives.

Yankee looked on as Suzanne, Wil and Jan walked out of the bar.

III

Attempted Murder in Mexico
By Marcello Barcqe

MEXICO CITY — Today in a northern province of Mexico, an attempt to kill a high-ranking USDEA official was foiled by Mexican authorities. Sources close to the investigation told this reporter that the assassination attempt failed because agents conducting a countersurveillance operation detected the plot early in the preparation stages and federal police allowed it to proceed far enough to establish irrefutably both the conspiracy to commit the act and execution of the act itself. Commissioner Martín Santos praised the police for their daring confrontation of a vicious drug cartel on its home ground.

THE BRASS PLAQUE READS: Garmeister McCaffey and Stoddard. It is discreetly displayed at the entrance to a renovated early 20th-century, corner bank building in a quiet DC suburb retaining the historic landmark exterior and masking 21st-century information technology the likes of which existed only in NSA. Old, richly appointed in the style of yesteryear, but more modern in function than all but the top one-thousandth of one percent of similar firms in the world.

For the world is Garmeister McCaffey and Stoddard's realm, international contracting and finance its game, and old-fashioned competence, demeanor and discretion its trademarks. Capable of conducting all its legal and financial services in-house, Garmeister McCaffey and Stoddard (GMS as it is known in the close quarters of the trade) is the first choice for many top-tier international corporations, sovereign governments, and non-profit and governmental organizations across the globe. The first two floors of the sedate building contain the reception and staff areas; the third floor, the private offices and conference rooms of the three principals. The office and vaults below ground level, however, are the exclusive preserve of Simon Stoddard; he alone controls access to a world not shared with his partners, associates, and clients in the three floors above.

Simon Stoddard and one of his clandestine associates, Amos Sanson, were seated in Simon's private sanctuary, deep in conversation. In a wide-ranging exchange, they discussed terrorist tactics, drug cartels, ALF/ELF and a conspiracy involving locally coordinated attacks in the United States by independent elements of the three acting together at the grassroots. Simon described a DEA proposal to protect a US diplomat who was being targeted by the triumvirate for promoting cooperation between US and Mexican authorities to prevent such attacks. During the conversation, Sanson decided to reveal Rosada Ángel Jesús's role as research and analysis specialist for a protective intelligence team employing her, Devon Xander as investigator, and himself as countersurveillance specialist.

"Amos, this may not be the right time to change your spots. You have amassed an influential following for your current path. It may not be the one least followed, but it has been a very good one for you."

"And for you, Simon."

"Yes, and for me too."

"The last time we talked, I told you I intended to pursue a new line, and now is the time."

"Are you sure the time is right, particularly given your standing in the Community?"

"Simon, for such a change as this, is the time ever right? Perhaps . . . it is simply . . . the time."

"Don't visit that philosophical mumbo-jumbo on me, Amos. We've ridden together into too many sunsets."

"Only to awaken to the new dawn of the same day. I have been mulling this over for quite a while. Though it may appear 'spur of the moment' it is not. I am older and hopefully wiser now, and definitely a step slower." Holding up his gloved hand, Sanson continued, "This hand remains useful, but dexterity and strength are waning; specialists advise me that decline is inevitable though total loss is not expected. Both body and mind tell me *now* is the time to begin the transition. Our services are still marketable, and I think Xander and Rosada will add to our effectiveness. Perhaps the return will diminish a bit initially, but we will make it up in sustainability. In part, it is an investment in capacity, and in part it is my way of managing risk. Xander needs a little more seasoning, and Rosada needs to sharpen some old tools and, perhaps, acquire some new ones. When an acquaintance was asked some time ago why he didn't quit, he replied that he was always going to step aside when he completed his current project, but by the time the current project was finished, he was deeply immersed in the next one . . ."

"And he couldn't . . . or wouldn't . . . quit . . ."

"You are correct, Simon, but then you usually are. The project you describe will require more than I alone can do, and the operational demands fit our resources and intent to develop them. The day will come when I can't stand alone against the storm. For that inevitable day, we must prepare now."

Swiveling his chair 90 degrees left, Simon fixed his eyes upon an exquisite Escheresque print—the *Deus Ex Machina*—paused momentarily, then said, "OK Amos, tell me what you have in mind . . . no detail yet, just a brief synopsis."

"Simon," Sanson began, leaning forward in his chair with a rare display of zeal, "we develop a protective intelligence unit, employing Rosada, Xander and me doing what we do best to protect our client. There are three functions required, and we are professionally qualified to carry them out. We prepare for the project together; but, when we go operational, Xander and I will do the fieldwork while Rosada supports us with research and communications. She will be especially useful in responding to our questions as the activity progresses. Negotiating the conditions and compensation for our services remains with you. You and I will reserve long-term commitments to Xander and Rosada until both of us are satisfied that the association is sound and they have demonstrated mastery during actual operations. We will begin simply and advance to more complex projects only if we, you and I, agree.

We will go no further if our assessment of project outcomes is not positive."

After a quiet moment, Simon turned to Amos, "I've got it for the moment, Amos. In 15 minutes, I must meet with some folks upstairs. Let's continue this discussion day after tomorrow about noon . . . I'll provide lunch. At that time, present in writing a succinct description of your proposal, including enough detail concerning your colleagues that I can appreciate their contributions. I must be able to understand the capabilities of the team if I am to estimate the allowable scope and scale of operations and equate resources with mission requirements when I negotiate with our clients."

Two days later, after a pleasant lunch, Simon and Amos returned to their conversation.

Presenting to Simon a memorandum responsive to his request, Amos briefed him on its contents, outlining in formal terms a business plan for the association and an action plan for the DEA operation. After responding to Stoddard's pointed questions, Sanson concluded, "Simon, with this project, we can both meet the requirements of DEA's request and field test our association with Devon and Rosada. I will make no commitments to them until, and unless, you and I agree that the business plan is sound and our implementation of the action plan warrants continuation of the team. If the concept does not prove worthy, we will simply continue as we have, perhaps engaging them on occasions when their talents fit our needs."

"Amos, we have a few days before a response to DEA is due. Your proposal appears sound, but this is a significant decision, so I need to think hard about it. I will call you at the bookstore no later than 2359 tomorrow, saying simply go or no-go. A 'no-go' means I am unable to negotiate compensation sufficient to employ your team and we will not undertake this activity. A 'go' recommendation will extend only to this DEA inquiry. Later, we will continue our discussion of the future. Do you approve?"

"I do."

After a few minutes of small talk, Simon returned to his third-floor office and Amos became once again the quiet bookseller returning home after a routine buying trip. The next day, at precisely 2359, a message arrived: "Go."

A few days later, at the coffee table in Rosada's bookstore, Amos Sanson and Devon Xander sipped coffee while their hostess prepared a pleasantly aromatic tea before returning to their conversation. Sanson had completed his briefing for the security detection mission in Mexico. During the briefing, Xander and Rosada had listened intently and asked a few salient questions. They offered comments concerning the action plan and their roles in the operation.

"As I understand it," Xander began, "I shall investigate the routes and buildings, and work directly with the authorities and principals. My activity, though discreet, will be overt and in keeping with my experience as a policeman. You, Amos, will covertly watch for hostile surveillance, and Rosada will back up our fieldwork with research and analysis from here. We will stay in contact through secure communications arranged by someone we don't know but whom Amos trusts implicitly. No information will be sent through the system except in strict accordance with the protocols."

"And my part," began Rosada, "will be to assist with the initial portfolios, ferret out information in response to your inquiries from the field, and send it during the times shown in the protocol. My research will include both open and private sources, acquiring as much as possible through contacts generally available to sophisticated reference librarians and smoothing out the landscape with salient items from private contacts. I am not responsible for getting the operational computer, nor am I to be concerned with its removal following closure. How do you know it will be secure in my shop?"

"During my previous visit here, my logistical needs were met without my knowing how," replied Sanson. "We simply rely upon the same level of support." Addressing both Xander and Rosada, he continued, "You may wish to begin gathering information immediately. You have the mission schedule and should make such arrangements as you think appropriate. We will not meet again until after the operation, though in strict accordance with the plan, we will be in contact. If all seems well to you, let's turn the conversation to best sellers and favorite classics."

Malcolm Garfield's family tree included a US president and senior policy makers at both state and federal levels. Malcolm was a federal senior civil service drug administration investigator, up through the ranks, street-smart, capable. He trusted Simon Stoddard's recommendation of Devon Xander for the surveillance detection operation for his coming meeting with Mexican federal police, but he always checked with his own sources. Trust but verify: a very useful hand-me-down from a popular US politician.

Xander was raised in small border towns in southwestern Texas. After Army military police service and attendance at the Texas police academy, he joined the El Paso police force. Because of his fluency in Spanish and knowledge of Latino community life, Xander was assigned to an organized crime task force headed by the US Border Patrol where he quickly gained a reputation for solid police work. In parallel, he remained in the Army reserves, first as a non-commissioned officer then as a commissioned officer. Currently, he is a USAR major. He deployed to Kosovo, then to the Middle East and southern Central Asia, serving on and commanding MP mobile training teams working with local authorities. His current security clearances are at a level commensurate with Malcolm's needs. About a year ago, he was involved in a shootout that left him and a patrolman on his Midwestern city police force wounded and four dead bodies on the ground. Garfield was confident that Stoddard's recommendation was sound.

Though Garfield's schedule had not yet been announced, Devon Xander had been on the ground in Mexico for several days. Garfield would be in and out quickly, limiting his exposure to danger to a very short time. The surveillance detection team had to do its work before Garfield's arrival.

After establishing his bona fides with local officers directing the operational security component, Xander verified the information in the reports that he and Rosada had reviewed and updated prior to his move into the operational area. With his Mexican counterparts, and on his own, he visited the buildings in which Garfield was to stay and the meeting was to take place, and he drove and walked the routes between them. He checked the likely attack locations along the routes and inside the buildings, and investigated the probable surveillance locations from which attackers could watch Garfield and his protection detail, and the locations from which the protection detail could keep track of what was happening in and around the surveillance locations; all standard procedure, and likely known by the alarmingly sophisticated intelligence apparatus of the cartel. Watchers watched watchers in a never-ending game. But pre-operation surveillance was thought to be the weakest link in the cartel's attack cycle, so surveillance detection was taken very seriously on both sides of the line.

Xander was in his element, doing what he did best. He did not feel alone. His reports went to Rosada daily, and information came to him as well. He knew that Sanson was out there somewhere, quietly watching for anyone lurking in places not on the official lists and lines of sight unexplored by the protection details, and for anyone watching Xander as he worked. Like a skilled fly-fisher, Sanson would have his hand on the line and would know when to set the hook. The tingle Xander always felt when engaged was there. He knew that he was exposed to danger and he always tried to be aware of his surroundings. Still, the tingle was there, and Xander relished every moment of it.

Sanson was there. He was one of those unique people who could move through a neighborhood without causing a ripple. Local folks did not notice him; street people—merchants and vendors, mothers with small children, regulars in the bars, cafés, parks and plazas—did not react to his presence. Street toughs demanded reaction from the people, they caused ripples; eyes followed them and people on the street shied away from them. Often, Sanson detected their presence by observing the reactions of the locals; he "saw" strangers by following their ripples. And he knew that the mission surveillance mounted by terrorists and criminals would employ some locals, including policemen, but eventually the professionals would check the scene personally. So, he watched.

Sanson checked the same features that Xander investigated, and he checked Xander as he investigated. By observing his colleague and reading his daily reports to Rosada, Sanson was appraising Xander's operational capabilities, vetting him for a longer-term association. Simon Stoddard was a critical evaluator; Sanson knew he would have to provide solid evidence of Xander's fitness if the team he envisioned was to become a part of Stoddard's network. Pre-deployment research and analysis had strengthened Sanson's conviction that he, Devon Xander and Rosada Ángel Jesús could work well together. So far, their working relationship was functioning well in the field. But, the proof of the pudding was yet to come. If something happened to Malcolm

Garfield during his stay in Mexico, Sanson's mission would be judged a failure, Stoddard's reputation would be tarnished, and Sanson's team would not materialize as he envisioned it. So, he watched.

Hints of Garfield's visit began to surface in Mexico City. A well-connected journalist, Marcello Barcqe, in an article focused on the involvement of federal police in cartel security operations, mentioned that a high-level meeting between Mexican and US Drug Enforcement officials was coming soon. The location and timing were not specified, but speculation centered on major border-crossing cities in northern Mexico. Barcqe assured his readers that he would cover the story and publish a full account of the meeting.

US authorities were not pleased with the revelation because they knew that, given time, the cartels were likely to ferret out preparations for a meeting on their home grounds and discover when and where it would take place. Garfield was confident, however, that his precautions, including the covert operation arranged with Simon Stoddard, would secure his safety and assure a successful exchange of information with the Mexicans.

As Sanson watched, and as Xander's reports summarized the results of the Mexican and USDEA surveillance detection activities, ripples appeared and a pattern of activity emerged, though it was vague and required constant verification. Subtle activity was detected near the surveillance locations and occasional visitors caused surreptitious glances among the regular inhabitants of the streets and plazas between the discreet neighborhood and the fortress-like Federal

Building that were the center of Sanson and Xander's surveillance detection activities.

Xander was the first to report to Rosada that several new US security people had joined the US–Mexican protective team. Then Sanson and Xander reported increased police presence in and around the buildings where Garfield's party would be staying and the meeting with Mexican officials was scheduled, and along the route between them. Rosada suggested that the level of activity indicated that the time for Garfield's arrival was fast approaching. Not long after, Sanson noticed new people near several of the surveillance locations along the routes. At certain times during the day, he saw tourists with cameras. Occasionally at night they reappeared, and seemed to be jotting down notes in pocket notebooks. All this was reported by Xander to the commander of the protective force, without attribution beyond his own observations.

Both Sanson and Xander believed that cartel intelligence was following the changes in US–Mexican protective activities and stepping up their surveillance in response. They suspected that the cartel was making final preparations for an assault on Garfield's party as it moved between their lodging and the Federal Building. Where and when the attack would occur remained in doubt, but Sanson's observations that one route was receiving more intense scrutiny suggested a higher level of danger there. During the last few hours, activity at surveillance locations from which the entrances and exits to Garfield's lodgings could be seen seemed to be intensifying as well.

Included among these locations were two points affording excellent fields of fire for snipers.

Xander recommended to protective force command that they either secure these positions or allow continuation of the activity, expecting to discover the acute danger in time to ensure Garfield's safety and catch any snipers red-handed. Taking the positions away would not necessarily eliminate the threat; criminals and terrorists often simply abort for the time being or check to plan B. But, allowing their use and preparing a decisive counterstroke could keep the positions in police gunsights, provide an air-tight case for the public prosecutor, and if successful, seriously dampen the cartel's influence in the community.

Protective force command had a difficult risk analysis ahead of them, and Malcolm Garfield was not particularly keen to be bait dangling on a hook.

No matter how thorough the preparation, it still surprises:

Heavy trucks smashed into the motorcade, cutting off Garfield's armored SUV inside a kill zone from which escape appeared impossible. Quickly, the vehicle turned toward the only path open, and accelerated; but, after a few feet, it was suddenly lifted off the street by a huge explosion that left a crater into which it fell mangled and in flames.

The protective detail responded, quickly occupying the surveillance and attack locations, and securing the area surrounding the explosion. Mexican federal police SWAT teams rounded up the few people in or near the surveillance and attack locations, and secured two square blocks around the burning SUV. A forensic team stood by, awaiting orders to enter the crime scene. An hour later, they approached the wreckage and began their investigation.

Xander and Garfield's US protective detail slowly approached the crater and looked down at the still smoldering wreckage. They saw what had been a sewer beneath the street and talked quietly, almost admiringly, about the craftsmanship displayed by the crater and the destroyed armored car. Shaking his head, the Secret Service agent standing beside Xander turned and gestured. Surrounded by heavily armed Mexican federal police officers, Malcolm Garfield and Commissioner Martín Santos walked to the gaping hole, peered down at the blackened mass of twisted metal, exchanged a few words with the commander of the protective detail, then moved on to complete their discussions.

Weeks of preparation by Mexican and American drug administration authorities, and the drug cartel, culminating in fiery violence, followed by business as usual.

True to his word, Marcello Barcqe dispatched a detailed account to his Mexico City newspaper.

Two days later, Devon Xander bid good-bye to his Latino colleagues and left Mexico. And Sanson? Xander alone had any idea of his whereabouts.

As a glowing sun descended into the peaceful ocean off Casco Viejo, Amos Sanson and Devon Xander gazed west from the second-floor balcony of the Meridor Café, sipped light red wine of local vintage and

discussed in hushed tones the events of the past fort-
night. On the table between them lay Marcello Barcqe's
articles describing the assassination attempt and featuring interviews with Mexican and US officials along
the border and in Mexico City. They agreed that Barcqe
knew people in high places, was discreet in attribution
and comfortable with details, and clearly understood
the broader context. Gaps covering some sensitive
issues were sprinkled throughout the accounts, however, leading them to wonder what he might be trading
for access to sources and protection from corrupt and
vengeful elements within and outside the government.

Xander, as if talking to himself, said, "We found
the EOD team responsible for checking the sewer in
shallow graves in the church meditation yard. They
died about the same time the bomb exploded, but they
weren't killed by the blast. They were double tapped,
.22 long rifle rounds in the back of the head. We think
they planted a charge designed to shoot up through the
thin sewer roof, and then command detonated it from
a perch in the steeple. Chalk marks were found on the
pavement debris. The SUV was channeled over the
marks by the two trucks. They knew the driver would
take evasive action, so they gave him a quick way out
and . . ."

"I am not surprised by the precision of the attack.
They failed in their purpose, however. Garfield succeeded. No doubt the collateral damage shook the
community, but Martín Santos will see it right." After
a brief pause, Sanson pointed to Marcello Barcqe's
articles with a noticeably tremulous gloved hand and
continued, "Barcqe's accounts, though somewhat

flawed, seem sensible. An astute journalist can ferret out much; Marcello Barcqe appears astute . . . and connected. We may want to follow his career closely. In seven days, we shall share experiences with Ms. Jesús, and draw operational lessons for the future. Until then, mi amigo, vaya con Dios."

Tomorrow, Xander would return to his role as police chief, but for the moment he found comfort in the gathering night. Amos Sanson had already merged with the darkness.

Sanson and Xander sipped coffee while Rosada prepared tea. When she resumed her place at the table, Sanson nodded and she continued, "The pace at which information flowed was demanding but manageable. I was able to respond to all your questions, but providing clear estimates of probabilities for uncertainties at the times required by the protocols was, at times, challenging. If we are to engage in more complex projects, I'll need more time. The equipment functioned perfectly and was, as you promised, Amos, here and gone without a trace. It was the best I have ever used."

Sanson turned his attention to Devon Xander, "I had no difficulty covering the operational area, and the US and Mexican protective units were well-trained and professional. Cooperation was far better than I anticipated. The information provided by you, Rosada, kept me a step ahead; that contributed a lot, I think, to the positive reception accorded me by the protective teams. But, I was surprised by the EOD turncoats. Identifying the bandits before they hit is difficult, especially when they are with us daily. And the level of expertise displayed in the attack was sobering. Mexican federal police arrested more than twenty-seven, but only four—two two-man sniper teams—were caught red-handed; they were taken without incident before Garfield and Santos were allowed into the blast zone. We may have been lucky that a second bomb aimed at first responders was not used."

Then Sanson described the operation as it unfolded while he watched. During a lengthy discussion, the three collated their observations and activities. Several hours later, they completed their review and Amos left the bookstore. Rosada and Xander talked a while longer, agreeing that working with Amos Sanson was exacting . . . and exhilarating. Then Xander crossed the street to his office, and Rosada locked the shop door and went upstairs to her newly renovated apartment.

Seated in a comfortable chair in his subterranean sanctum, Simon Stoddard faced Amos Sanson and began, "Malcolm was quite pleased with the project and Xander's contribution. The explosion was unfortunate, but it was presented to the public as resulting from a gas leak in an aging sewer main, and it caused no material damage to the tasks at hand. Indeed, Martín Santos believes that political leaders on both sides of the border, fearful of the growing sophistication exhibited by the attack, will now harden their opposition to the drug cartels, leading to greater cooperation and allocation of resources. What is your appraisal, Amos?"

Pacing his words, Sanson replied, "I know little about the politics, Simon; however, I concur with Garfield's favorable view of Xander's performance.

He fit well into the protective force, furnished useful information to Ms. Jesús and me, and supplied valuable intelligence and expertise to the allied investigators. He stayed generally within his guidelines, but on occasion judiciously exercised professional initiative. I judge his performance as quite acceptable and am comfortable with our increasing the complexity of our next venture. Ms. Jesús operated the hub with the high degrees of competence and craftiness we anticipated, and she was satisfied with the logistics you arranged. Simon, I believe we are ready to go online."

"Well then, Amos, let us discuss a little matter that has come to my attention. I think it will require all the acumen we can bring to it."

IV

Sunday Sentinel Book Reviews

WASHINGTON, DC — Tomorrow, at the weekly luncheon of Washington's chapter of the National Press Club, Marcello Barcqe, award-winning journalist based in Mexico City, will discuss his frightening new book, Nexus: Cartel Cash, Terrorist Tactics, and Social Angst, *the dramatic account of a growing threat to the American homeland. Based on extensive research, including one-on-one interviews with many figures on both sides of the law, Barcqe has woven facts and expert opinions into a tale that both terrifies and titillates.* Nexus *is reviewed by Seymour Dexter in Sunday's* Review of Contemporary Literature, *which also features an article by Barcqe.*

AT THE SUNSET of a beautiful day in Casco Viejo, Amos Sanson sat contentedly sipping a light red wine of local vintage. He often sought refuge in Panama from the daily routine of the bookshop proprietor; it was a quick trip over familiar pathways that he looked forward to, along with book fairs and buying expeditions, with alacrity. Turning toward approaching footsteps, he recognized a familiar figure.

"You do not appear surprised to see me."

"The passage of time, Mr. Barcqe, brings much that is new but little that surprises."

Pointing to the chair opposite him, Sanson continued, "You reported an explosion caused by the accumulation of gas in an aging sewer. Your reputation for veracity suggests that you do not often shade the facts. Why, I have since wondered, did you choose to do so on that occasion?"

"Each of us, Mr. Sanson, has reasons to prefer privacy lest they cease to serve our best interests. On this occasion, however, I appear at the request of a mutual acquaintance to discuss an urgent matter and to convey his invitation to visit him. Shall I relate to you the tale that roused his concern?"

"Por favor."

"About a year ago, a US Border Patrol undercover agent, a young Latina named Mara de Jesús, was found partially exposed in a shallow grave on the US side of the border near Nogales. Her body displayed the marks of prolonged torture. Ms. de Jesús was part of an international investigation into rumors that a drug cartel had approached a Spanish terrorist organization with a proposal to fund training for an anti-abortion group in the United States that wished to commit arson, bombing, and if necessary, assassination among abortion advocates and clinical facilities on both sides of the Mexico–US border. I believe that this rumor was the focus of the Santos–Garfield meeting . . . supposition on my part but believed by important people in your country and mine. The trail from de Jesús's grave led to another shallow grave in which three low-level cartel enforcers were found. Mexican authorities believe that the three were executed by the cartel because their actions brought unwanted scrutiny at a time when a major cross-border drug movement was being planned. Mara de Jesús had a very close relative living in a small university city . . . her aunt, Rosada Ángel Jesús, is a friend of Devon Xander, local police chief, who was an integral part of the security force for the Santos–Garfield meeting. Ángel Jesús retired from US federal service after distinguished assignments in Latin America and is owner of a rental property known to have been occupied briefly by a quiet gentleman whose right hand was sheathed in a color-coordinated cloth glove even during sultry weather . . . a gentleman with whom she shares a professional interest in books."

Barcqe paused.

"Interesting. You appear quite confident in your story."

"I am a noted, in some circles renowned, journalist, Mr. Sanson, and, as I believe you know, integrated into various networks within which such stories circulate. Included among my acquaintances is an equally well-networked gentleman: Mr. Simon Stoddard. He suggested that you might be interested in my story, and he asked that I convey to you his invitation to meet at noon two days hence in his sanctum. And now, Mr. Sanson, I must depart to prepare for . . ."

". . . an interview tomorrow with the constructor responsible for increasing the capacity of the Canal."

As he rose, Marcello Barcqe smiled and raised his glass in silent salute. A moment later, he emerged from the Meridor and crossed the street as a large SUV approached. From the shadows of a doorway, a well-dressed imposing man emerged, glanced casually up and down the street, opened the back door of the SUV and followed Barcqe inside.

As the sun dipped below the horizon, Amos Sanson mused, sipped his wine and thought about . . .

It is often difficult to penetrate the quiet watchman's mind.

Two days later, at precisely noon, Sanson selected a small gourmet sandwich, poured a cup of coffee, and seated himself across from Simon Stoddard. Slowly he ate, then drank, watching as Stoddard stared at his computer monitor. Abruptly, Simon stroked a few keys, hit "enter" with a flourish and turned to greet Amos. "Welcome old friend. I trust you and Marcello had a fruitful exchange."

"He is an interesting conversationalist."

"Coming directly from a meeting with Malcolm Garfield, Marcello brought me unsettling news, and the prospect of a complex but intriguing project. Garfield wants us to look into a pressing concern near Nogales."

"Garfield seems constantly pressed by one thing or another. But, he deals in significant matters, so . . ."

"Both Garfield's intelligence and Barcqe's contacts indicate that a major cross-border movement of illicit narcotics is being planned. It involves, so the information suggests, multiple crossings, elaborate diversions and a nexus of interests that could be devastating. Government response to such an operation requires the commitment of many resources at substantial cost; the command and control apparatus alone is daunting and standing up the military and police forces on both sides of the border may not be possible without such an array of signatures that tipping our hand cannot be avoided. Garfield wants to nip it in the bud, but not before an actionable conspiracy case can be brought. Marshaling the necessary forces is costly, and the standby expenses are high; so, authorities are reluctant to commit at current levels of uncertainty. As usual, the balance is precarious, so stealth is essential. Garfield believes that a low-profile effort can acquire sufficient evidence to convince higher authorities to support prosecution of a conspiracy case, and if necessary, upset the diversionary nexus and allow the military and law enforcement folks to deal with the border crossings. Interested?"

"Being interested and being willing are often different. I have no doubt that Rosada Jesús can handle the research and information requirements, but whether Xander and I can meet the demands in the field is at issue. Xander's previous success is encouraging, but his activity was overt. Whether we can move him completely into the shadows is questionable; not impossible, but questionable. I had hoped for another mission that I could watch over. This, however, will require full commitment for both of us. Have I time to formulate an action plan for your perusal?"

"Amos, at noon three days from today, I must respond to Garfield."

"I need all summary analyses, including conclusions, compiled by Garfield and Barcqe."

"All they will share is in this briefcase. They assure me that it is substantive and expertly analyzed. Sources are expunged but nearly all is independently corroborated, uncertainties are quantified or described using standard terms, and unanticipated influences and uncertain out-comes are discussed; it is the best they can do."

"I will return well before the deadline. At this stage, Simon, life should have become a bit simpler."

At 0900 three days later, Amos Sanson began, "The project Malcolm Garfield proposes is comprised of three complex elements, any one of which would be suitable for us, but the whole is too much for us to undertake. The information in the briefcase is exten-sive and will enable us to successfully complete one of the elements: protective surveillance of the Nogales abortion clinic."

"Why do you think that is the one?"

"It involves a stationary target on a city street in a low traffic area affording both surveillance and coun-tersurveillance perches and does not require that we cross an international border. Recently, both Xander and I completed international missions that exposed us to formal identity checks when crossing borders, and I think a little more time should pass before we risk another trip through Homeland Security and other border scrutiny. Perhaps more importantly, the scale and scope of the operation lie well within the capabili-ties of one person; Xander can do this by himself with-out undue risk. Demonstrations are not uncommon at this location and Malcolm has monitored them well, so we have a sound baseline. Rosada can support the activity. She and Devon are well versed in the context and will be briefed on the possible connection with Malcolm's larger picture. I shall watch over the oper-ation, but Xander will not know I'm there. Rosada will keep me in the communications net, but she will not know that I am near Xander. This is a final test, Simon; after this, you may have another confirmed asset capable of independent action."

"Malcolm Garfield has confidence in Xander, so that should not be a hard sell. Fill me in."

Two hours later, Amos rose to leave, pausing as Simon dialed Garfield's private number. After a brief conversation, Simon hung up the phone and turned toward Amos. With a theatrical voice framed in a sly smile, he said, "The game's afoot."

A day later, cups of coffee and tea upon the table in Rosada's bookstore, Amos read Rosada and Devon into the operation.

At the same time, in a remote hacienda somewhere in Mexico, the heads of three drug cartels believed by Mexican and US authorities to be locked in genocidal war for dominance in the North American narcotics market were sitting down to the latest of their periodic conferences.

On the streets, their soldiers were engaged in local battles for the retail trade. But at the chief executive level, the three cartels had formed a consortium, supported by private military forces capable of standing toe to toe with almost any light infantry or special operations forces their size in the world. The sophisticated organization surpassed credulity among the politically-appointed policy makers on both sides of the border.

Guarded by a thousand-meter moat of grass no higher than a man's knees patrolled by fighting bulls conditioned to hate men, within a walled complex secured as only the highest levels in military and law enforcement intelligence organizations, the three leaders, accompanied by just their most trusted lieutenants, chatted casually before opening the meeting to an agenda of unusual complexity. They were planning an operation that would combine their money with terrorist trainers and generally well-meaning social activists in an end run around Mexican and US border security forces to move the largest single shipment of illicit drugs ever attempted into the bottomless market north of the border. And, pressed by increasingly active anti-drug operations, they were looking for a grand score before relocating their executive operations into the more easily managed countries between Mexico and Costa Rica.

At this stage, they were hoping for a much simpler life for themselves and their families.

Amos Sanson looked closely. Lillian de Vizcaya? Why? Delving into aging memories, Sanson searched for connections with the current situation. Lillian de Vizcaya did not appear in the briefing documents furnished by Simon Stoddard and Malcolm Garfield. She was from a bygone era, from a time before Sinn Fein was accepted as a legitimate political actor on the Irish stage. Irish? Of course, "Irish Jack" Kavanaugh! A constant companion of the vivacious Irish-born Basque separatist, Jonathon Cotswold Kavanaugh, twice arrested but never convicted, was an ideologically motivated master planner—and, some believed, master bomb maker—for the Irish Republican Army during earlier rounds between the IRA and the UK.

Deliberately, the connection emerged from Sanson's mind: An Irish-Catholic ideologue, Irish Jack's presence near demonstrations outside an abortion clinic made some sense, but his right-or-wrong conscience insulated him from the despicable trade in illicit drugs. The perfect foil, Kavanaugh could be an unwitting accomplice in a cartel deception plan.

Very carefully, Sanson followed de Vizcaya. Her tradecraft was not the best, but Nogales was not Belfast or London. So, he moved carefully.

An hour and a half later, his patience paid off. Seated outside a small cantina in the barrio, an aging Irish Jack sipped alternately from a wine glass and a small cup. Sanson watched Lillian stroll past the cantina and round the corner at the end of the street. A few minutes later, she appeared in the cantina doorway, then disappeared with Kavanaugh into the bar. Sanson did not follow them into the cantina. A gringo in a barrio bar did not escape suspicion. For now, knowing they were here was enough.

Sanson waited under the trees, but they did not immediately come out. Aware that his idle presence would draw attention, he backed off and called Rosada. Within minutes, the sighting was correlated into their growing database and forwarded to SCION, aka Malcolm Garfield, who added the information to his list of indications that the cartel operation probably was underway.

Immediately upon learning that Kavanaugh and de Vizcaya were in Nogales, Malcolm Garfield directed one of his analysts to review their MOs. Within the hour, the analyst returned to brief Garfield.

Irish Jack specialized in property destruction with no attendant deaths, though occasional collateral damage brought casualties. Generally, his intent was to draw police, military, and other first responders away from higher priority targets that were to be attacked by others. He was, of course, equally as guilty as an active participant in the operations, but though jailed several times, Kavanaugh had not been convicted of killing anyone. He was cast as a courageous ideologue with firm convictions against murder and assassination. Often, he stood nose-to-nose against IRA gunmen without flinching, but he was devoted to the cause.

Lillian de Vizcaya was different. Born of Irish and Basque parents and raised among a mixture of opposition intellectuals and stone-cold killers, she was volatile, brilliant, and brave to the point of recklessness. When younger, de Vizcaya was more likely to stand with the guns, but now she was devoted to Kavanaugh and to his cause.

Conclusion: Together, they were formidable, but thought to be reasonably predictable. They were probably not in Nogales to kill people, but to provide fireworks to divert attention from the drug kingpins' cross-border operation. If Kavanaugh were threatened, he would defend himself, but de Vizcaya would seek out and destroy anyone who threatened him. She was a clear danger to Xander.

Garfield sent Xander instructions to check on Kavanaugh and de Vizcaya, but not to take unnecessary risks.

The test Sanson and Stoddard had set for Xander was ratcheting up.

Feeling secure behind the moat of grass, the Consortium finished an important meeting. Within days, authorities in and around Nogales would be inundated with emergency calls reporting explosions of natural gas lines and gasoline filling stations throughout the area. The emergencies would occur seemingly at random, drawing all public safety and gas utility resources to widely scattered sites and occupying all investigative and disaster management resources in attempts to get a handle on the event. Roads and streets would be jammed with emergency vehicles, and detours would confuse motorists. In the chaos, two bombs would be detonated at an abortion clinic. The first would be a small bomb in the clinic lab that would force evacuation of the clinic. The second would be a larger blast with a fire accelerant placed to completely engulf the structure within minutes. One clinic destroyed, no significant casualties.

At the first reports of disaster in Nogales, bulldozers at construction sites on the Mexican side of the border, two east and one west of Nogales, would drive through the protective fence in remote areas within the greater Nogales region. They would be followed by convoys of off-road vehicles loaded with narcotics. After clearing the fence, the heavy pickups and all-wheel-drive vans would fan out along the trails and roads that interlaced the deserted backcountry. Soon they would be beyond the area patrolled locally to prevent relatively low volumes of infiltration through the region. Some would not get through, but the Consortium believed the amount of product that did get through would be the largest single shipment of drugs ever to enter the US market, in itself a major victory.

The event was planned for late afternoon or early evening so the chaos would occur during the afternoon rush hours and the border-crossing elements would soon be cloaked in darkness. Risky? Yes, but potentially high return. After this success, the Consortium high command would withdraw to relative safety in Central America.

Report Nbr 03 CONFIDENTIAL TO SCION

1730 10-Instant: Tracy Owen entered cantina (photo attached). Source reports he passed through the bar into the storeroom. On legitimate pretext, inside source entered the storeroom. Owen was not in the storeroom, nor had he exited the cantina by the back door.

1830: Owen entered the bar from the storeroom and exited the cantina through the front entrance.

REPORT ENDS

Malcolm Garfield sent the photo to the identity division for verification. Owen was indeed the same Tracy Owen known to be a leader of the Saviors, a radical element of the Southwest Division of the American Chapter of the International Association for Anti-Abortion Advocacy. Garfield ordered a 24/7 stakeout on the cantina and 24/7 surveillance on Owen.

But, a mystery remained. After entering the cantina, where had Owen gone?

A plausible answer was provided by local police. During prohibition, the cantina was part of a small network of establishments linked by tunnels through which tequila was transported. With the end of prohibition and the passage of time, the tunnel system was forgotten. Perhaps it had been reopened for a similar purpose but a new product.

Four other bars were included in the original network; all four were still in business. Garfield ordered round-the-clock surveillance on all four. Within a week, each was visited by a different member of Savior.

The puzzle was filling in.

Report Nbr 12 CONFIDENTIAL TO SCION

2100 12-Instant: Kavanaugh and de Vizcaya entered the cantina.

2300: Owen entered the cantina. On legitimate pretext, inside source entered the storeroom and lower-level wine cellar; Owen was not there.

Similarly, simultaneous surveillance of Savior officers entering the other four bars in the network reports targets entering and disappearing.

0200 13-Instant: Owen exited cantina. Similarly, the other four surveillance targets exited their respective bars.

0300: Kavanaugh and de Vizcaya exited the cantina.

ASSESSMENT: We believe a major meeting was held in the tunnel system involving all targets, probably for final coordination of an attack or disruption of services at the clinic. This correlates with other agency reports of acquisition by Savior of enough materials to construct either one very large incendiary bomb or as many as 25 smaller bombs. Savior has had more than enough time to construct the bombs. We believe attack is imminent, within the next 12 to 36 hours.

RECOMMENDATION: Simultaneously take down all five (5) Savior cells ASAP!

REPORT ENDS

Garfield ordered the takedown. Twenty-four hours later, the cells were in custody, but EOD personnel reported that the amount of explosive material recovered was less than expected. They suspected that some bombs had already been placed. Based on information discovered during the raids, they began to search, but searching the number of potential targets for small bombs like those found in the extremists' arsenals was time-consuming activity.

At 16:12:46 hours, the phone rang in the call center of Nogales 911: A gasoline-dispensing pump in a downtown filling station was afire and threatened seven other pumps. Patrons reported that the fire was preceded by "a muffled boom." Rapid response was warranted, but it was treated as a routine emergency call. Within the next 103 minutes, five additional calls—two at filling stations and three at shopping mall natural gas meters—were registered. The periods between calls varied. The third similar call had spurred supervisors in the emergency operations center to initiate the city's disaster response plan and notify the mayor's office and the police and fire departments that a serious situation might be developing. The seventh and eighth calls for explosions and jetting fires at cutoff valves on a ten-inch gas transmission line near a heavily populated northwestern suburb convinced them that a major man-made incident was in play.

The alarm cascaded up through the regional emergency response system. The governor was alerted. Public safety units assumed control at critical points in the rush-hour traffic patterns, but movement within the city slowed. Streets were jammed; emergency vehicles had to creep through masses of irate drivers. Regional officials were convinced that something more sinister than coincidental or systemic failure was occurring in the natural gas distribution system.

Homeland Security picked up on the electronic chatter among the local authorities well before formal notification arrived.

Then a fire erupted in the medical laboratory of an abortion clinic, but the simultaneous occurrence of demonstrations at the clinic and fires scattered through the city had overwhelmed the city's emergency responders. Patients and staff evacuated the clinic without casualties, and firefighters entered to suppress the fire. A deafening explosion ripped through the clinic storeroom, engulfing the structure in fire and causing injuries to the firefighters and a few evacuees and bystanders. Emergency medical services and firefighting reinforcements could not respond because the streets were jammed with traffic. Clinic staff turned their attention to the casualties.

Within minutes of the last reports to 911, three bulldozers slammed through the chain link fence along the US–Mexico border near Nogales, clearing paths for convoys of trucks and vans. West of Nogales several vehicles were delayed or stopped, but east of the city, an unknown number of vehicles reached the rural tracks, trails, and roads leading north and east into the mountains. Occupants of the vehicles opened fire on the Border Patrol officers who attempted to stop the onslaught. The firefights forced the officers to deploy and engage in scattered battles all along the infiltration path. Dusk followed by nightfall—the convoys fanned out and disappeared into the darkness and the rough terrain.

Even before the alarm had passed up the chain of command from Nogales, Malcolm Garfield had read flash reports from Devon Xander, alerted his people, coordinated with the task-force agencies, and arranged both aerial surveillance of the area around Nogales and flights for himself and his field command staff to Tucson. He expected to be on the ground in force by first light. Local authorities, including backcountry experts from Native American reservation police and Arizona National Guard units trained especially for surveillance, interdiction and rescue in the rugged terrain, were already responding.

The cartel Consortium had planned a historic score, but Garfield had waited a long time to get at them on his ground.

Garfield met Xander at the airport in Tucson, and quickly integrated him into the federal command and control staff. Xander would be the liaison officer between Garfield's intelligence and operations unit and local police and National Guard operations centers. Xander's experience with local law enforcement and National Guard deployments was immediately put to good use. And Garfield wanted him nearby as his informal advisor.

Aerial surveillance and real-time satellite imagery had already observed several suspect activities. If they turned out to be elements of the Consortium invasion, firefights and hot pursuits were likely. Legitimate travelers would be informed of the situation and either directed to leave the area or detained until the area was cleared. Some of the mules would get through, but Malcolm Garfield was determined to limit the Consortium to less than their usual success rate. His goal was to contain them and to make their audacity so expensive that they would not attempt it again.

Xander was in constant motion, moving among O&I, police and military commands, and Garfield's headquarters. Garfield's authority went with him, so he could make decisions and resolve differences wherever he went.

Garfield's HQ was adjacent to the tactical operations center (TOC) from which the field operations were directed. The TOC was up 24/7, crammed with sophisticated communications equipment and surveillance monitors, and people conferring in small groups or scurrying from place to place. It was at the same time chaotic and controlled, quiet and cacophonous, and deadly serious. Radio traffic was generally confined to headsets, but occasionally something was fed to speakers so all could hear. Real-time surveillance imagery was generally limited to specialized monitors, but occasionally something was fed to a giant screen so all could see. Sections for Navaho police, designated "Hawk," National Guard ("Minuteman"), and USDEA ("Eagle"), were clearly marked. Deputy sheriffs, Nogales police detectives, and state police represented local and state law enforcement.

Xander moved constantly between the TOC and Garfield's headquarters. He paused to speak with someone, read a brief message or stare for a moment at a monitor. He listened as Hawk reported a positive bandit sighting and Minuteman moved to intercept. He watched the interception on a surveillance monitor and listened to the cheers when the bandit went down. And he carried the news, good or bad, to Garfield.

Garfield pretty much stayed in his HQ, nearby if needed, but out of the way of the professionals who were expert at their jobs. This was a tough time for him. Having set all this in motion, he had the good sense not to micromanage the battle, but he ached to get into the thick of it. More than once, Xander met him at the door, always with a piece of news or to relay a question that only Garfield could answer. Periodically, Garfield walked through the TOC, asked a question here or there, chatted momentarily with Xander, and returned to the HQ. Later, he was told by Xander how much the people appreciated Garfield's presence, and his leaving them alone to do their jobs.

Reviewing the operation at the end of the first 12 hours, it was apparent that a few successful intercepts had been accomplished. As the countryside cooled through the evening, thermal imagery revealed fewer vehicles moving through the operational area, and friend or foe indicators showed that nearly all were friendly. Whether some bandits were lying low or had passed beyond the cordon was unknown, but the attitude in Garfield's headquarters and the TOC was "confidently optimistic."

Behind the bulls on the hacienda, the Consortium quietly surveyed the results of the strike through the US border defenses.

"Initially," reported the Consortium intelligence officer, "the deception achieved its purpose and the penetration appeared to have succeeded. But, with the passage of time, the number of trucks and vans reporting they had reached points beyond the US response cordon is not reassuring. The operation will likely move a lot of product into the United States, but the record is slowly slipping away. The results appear to have been sufficient to reimburse the costs, but little or no money will be made."

They decided to rest and continue in the morning when more definitive information would be available. Just after dawn, 16 hours after launching their convoys, the Consortium reconvened around a sumptuous buffet to continue its review.

"News reports alternately chastised American authorities for 'allowing' the border penetration and praised them for their rapid response and apparently successful outcome. If we are patient, the gringo press will fill in many of the details, and our regular sources will provide salient insights.

"We are satisfied with the results of our collaboration with the Basque terrorists. The deception unfolded as they predicted: sufficient numbers of explosions and fires to distract the local first responders.

"In the primary assault, the bulldozers fulfilled their purpose, and our convoys achieved initial success. The confounding factor was the readiness of the state and federal forces. They marshaled more quickly than we anticipated. Operationally, we may achieve less than we hoped, but as an experiment, the attempt may reveal much."

"We never close our minds to the lessons presented," said the host. "We will conduct a thorough postmortem, and benefit from our successes and failures. There will be other opportunities. Let us begin the preparations now."

The leader of cartel operations in Sonora interjected, "I believe our project was compromised by the discovery of the dead Border Patrol officer. We have reviewed her time with us and are reasonably sure of the degree of her access to our planning. And with more details about the American actions, we can infer the content of her reports. Had we been able to interrogate her, we would have discovered exactly what she had conveyed to her superiors. Our three rogues deprived us of that opportunity, and the possibility of feeding the voracious appetite of Washington with misinformation. We think that at the very least she tipped our hand and the level of the US response reflected her warning."

Murmurs of assent passed among them as they turned their attention to breakfast. Later, they returned to the review, and to speculate about the future.

Near dawn after the second night of the incursion, Garfield and Xander, disheveled and wired by the spirit of the chase and caffeine, sat in the HQ reviewing status reports and talking about the detailed after-action review to come.

Looking at a handful of printouts, Xander said, "We brought down all five of Savior's three-man cells, but ten explosions with fire occurred and the community was pretty thoroughly disrupted. In the confusion, Kavanaugh and de Vizcaya slipped away. We don't have a line on them . . . yet.

"The initial assault on the fence was successful. Two corridors were opened and more than 90, maybe 100, off-road pickups and vans broke through. Mexican authorities were surprised at the number of vehicles assembled and their failure to detect the buildup. About three-quarters of the bandits passed east of Nogales and sprinted into the rough country to the northeast. The others passed west of the city into more populated areas. We stopped seven in that sector, but the difficulties in intercepts were exacerbated by pursuit in a more populous area.

"Preliminary thinking is that the thrust west of Nogales may have been part of a deception plan, along with the explosives and fires set by Savior. Following the breeches of the fence, we had lots of blips scattered west and northeast of Nogales.

"So far, we have intercepted about two-thirds of the blips to the east and north; about 15 of these intercepts were legitimate travelers who were detained for their safety. We are still receiving reports of hot intercepts.

"We've taken down 48 two-man mule teams and recovered their cargos; Drug Enforcement is assessing the take. And, some friendly casualties: two KIA and eighteen WIA so far. They came well armed—automatic weapons, hand grenades and two bandits used LAWS— and ready to fight . . . and win.

"For now, analysis suggests a well planned, financed and executed military-style operation. We have picked up soldiers from two cartels we thought were at each other's throats, and the use of terrorists and terrorist tactics multiplied their capabilities. Practical deception was employed, and their OPSEC was good. We responded effectively outside the city, and our admin/log support has kept us in action continuously. Pre-op surveillance and countersurveillance on this side tipped us to the operation, but not to its scale and timing. Currently, we think they have achieved only partial success because we put boots on the ground quickly. Hawk, Minuteman and the locals have performed very well.

"Malcolm, the full AAR will tell us a lot more, but, for now, I think the bad guys may have come to play a bigger game . . . maybe to test our capabilities. They may be sitting in a safe house somewhere evaluating the benefits and costs of operations combining their money and personnel with terrorist trainers and tactics, and deception built around social activism."

Malcolm Garfield had listened closely to Xander's report. He remained silent for several moments then, in a thoughtful mood, spoke up, "Your conclusion is sobering, Devon. And it suggests a new response level. A lot of people in DC think we are at war with drug cartels and terrorists, but, is it war, or good old-fashioned intelligence and police work? Maybe we can convince them to give us our own drones to keep real-time eyes on our remote border areas. Someday we might even locate that safe house and drop a little surprise package on those fat cats." His eyelids lowered and his chin sank onto his chest. Garfield slept.

"Tired and wired," Xander muttered to himself, "out-of-the-box thinking for a civil service wonk from

Justice, the Fed's bastion of conservative bureaucracy." Slowly, Xander shook the cobwebs from his head and walked over to the TOC.

Despite their aging, Lillian de Vizcaya and Jonathon Cotswold Kavanaugh remained sensitive to their surroundings. Situational awareness had carried them through many years of high-risk engagement. Though their work in Nogales was complete, they did not relax their guard. They began every contract with a thoughtful exit strategy. This one involved a middle-aged Arizona couple interested in vacationing south of the border.

Three weeks after the Nogales affair, a well-dressed couple entered a luxurious suite aboard a cruise ship in Los Angeles for a transit of the Panama Canal with stops along the way at Cabo San Lucas, Puerto Vallarta, Acapulco, Panama City, Cozumel, and Fort Lauderdale. It was a celebration of their first wedding anniversary. They had been happily looking forward to the trip for nearly six months.

When the ship docked for the day at Puerto Vallarta, they disembarked, strolled through the town and stopped at a café made famous by Robert James Waller in his book *Puerto Vallarta Squeeze*. After ordering, they went to the restrooms, returning minutes later to sit quietly, sip coffee and tequila, and return to the ship. Their personal identity and ship credentials were correct, so they were welcomed onboard. They continued the cruise, enjoying a beautiful day of scuba diving in Cozumel, and flew home from Fort Lauderdale to Phoenix. On Monday morning, they returned to work and delighted their fellow assistant prosecutors in the drug enforcement division of the state's department of justice with tales of sharks, rays and sea turtles sighted during the dives. Their colleagues were envious, and several vowed to undertake a similar excursion . . . when they could afford it.

In the meantime, a handsome couple traveled from Puerto Vallarta, through Guadalajara, to Mexico City, where they emplaned for Lisbon. In due time, they returned to a modest flat overlooking the Bay of Biscay. The next morning, to the greetings of old friends, they entered a neighborhood café for their usual café con leche, queso, and panecillos.

In pursuit of de Vizcaya and Kavanaugh, US authorities sought assistance from both Ireland and Spain, but the Irish reported no trace of them and Madrid hardly ever achieved success among the Basque.

As Amos Sanson placed his hand upon the ornate knob of Simon Stoddard's outer door following their routine after-action review, Simon said, "Amos, take some time to reconsider your inclination to retire. Xander has become a capable independent operative, but he is not you, nor will he ever, in my opinion, match your skills. He is a confidant of Malcolm Garfield, and that both qualifies him for and perhaps limits him to overt activities. People know of him and the roles he played in Mexico and Nogales. You and he complement each other, but he is not a substitute for you. Let's renegotiate your future, and the time, effort and compensation for continuance."

Thoughtfully, with eyes cast upon the Persian carpet at his feet, Sanson paused, then turned to look directly into Stoddard's eyes and nod slightly. At Stoddard's silent acknowledgment, he departed.

Simon smiled a bit, turned and moved his fingers toward the computer keyboard, then laced his fingers behind his head, leaned back in his chair, turned to his left, and gazed deeply into *Deus Ex Machina*. He sat quietly, thinking himself to have triumphed in this round with Amos Sanson. But, a thought intervened and he could not escape it. He simply had to admit his respect, admiration, and . . . yes . . . affection for the silent watchman.

Devon Xander and Amos Sanson had come to sit around the book-strewn table in Rosada's shop, sip coffee from brightly colored paper cups and share the terrible hurt as only those who know can share.

Memories flooded Rosada Ángel Jesús's mind as she alternately read Marcello Barcqe's account of Mara de Jesús's death and cried uncontrollably. Rosada remembered walking hand in hand with eleven-year-old Mara through the San Diego Zoo, laughing at the monkeys swinging from perch to perch, and Mara graduating from San Diego State with a bachelor's degree in criminal justice, and Mara receiving her badge and gun and being sworn into the US Border Patrol, and endless days and weeks and months when Mara was somewhere doing something that no one would talk about. And now her one and favorite Mara was dead.

Xander and Sanson were of a single thought: for this devastating blow, we will exact a heavy price. But for now, they sat in silence and shared the hurt.

V

Special to the *Panama City Daily Observer*

Three Deaths in Panama's Caribbean Free-Trade Zone a Mystery
By Marcello Barcqe

ZONA LIBRE COLON, PANAMA — Yesterday, the body of Joaquín Pretemo was discovered in a warehouse inside the free-trade zone, bringing to three the number of business executives found dead under unusual circumstances during the last month. The entire FTZ community is on edge because law enforcement officials believe that high ranking officers of international corporations are being targeted at random, leaving everyone to wonder who is next. Some say that the three commercial leaders were linked to a drug kingpin consortium responsible for a major border incursion into the United States that recently achieved limited success in the high stakes battle for supremacy in the US narcotics market.

SANSON AND XANDER were in the café early, seated in the rear left corner, their backs to the walls, where they could see both the front and rear entrances. They had already checked the neighborhood and the approaches from Kavanaugh and de Vizcaya's apartment.

When Irish Jack and Lillian entered, the barman greeted them with a nod directing their attention to the rear left corner. Kavanaugh and de Vizcaya glanced toward Sanson and Xander, de Vizcaya clearly showing a defensive attitude, but after the brief look, Kavanaugh smiled and walked directly to Sanson, extending his right hand. "Amos, much time has passed since last we were this close." Then turning to Xander, "Devon, old chum, the years since you left Belfast have served you well." Gesturing for Lillian to come forward, Jack said, "Lillian, come and say hello to our old friends."

Looking directly at Sanson as she approached, de Vizcaya said, "For an instant in Nogales, I thought I saw you, but I could not verify it."

Pointing to the right rear corner, Jack said, "Lillian, please play hostess for Devon. Amos and I have much to catch up on."

While the barman served first Kavanaugh and Sanson, then de Vizcaya and Xander, the other patrons moved to tables in the empty corner, leaving de Vizcaya and Xander with clear views (and fields of fire) encompassing the entrances and the room.

"Simon has occasionally placed us in the same theater, Amos, but never to sit in the same box. What path has he set that brings you into the north of Spain?"

"We have need of your special talents, Jack, and Simon is not along for this voyage, though I don't know him ever to be totally unaware of interests among his associates."

"Tell me, old . . . associate . . . what are our interests?"

"Devon and I are off the books for this one. We seek retribution for a hurt to a friend."

"Ms. Rosada Ángel de Jesús?"

"As perceptive as ever you were, old . . . associate."

"The lovely Mara. Unfortunate and unnecessary. Lillian and I did not know."

"Shall I continue?"

Irish Jack paused for a moment; then nodding and gesturing subtly to Lillian, he replied, "Por favor."

In the meantime, de Vizcaya and Xander had been fumbling with their breakfasts, each with eyes constantly moving, each aware of the other's hand hidden under the table. At Kavanaugh's gesture, de Vizcaya visibly relaxed, raised her hidden hand onto the table, and said, "We may as well be comfortable, Mr. Xander. I think we are going to be here for a while."

"Do you know that Pretemo is rumored to be Garfield's man?" asked Jack. "Mara was their link, and the three severed the link. But Pretemo did not know what they may have wrenched from her, so he killed them to protect himself."

"No, Jack, I did not know Pretemo might be linked with Garfield. If Garfield or Stoddard learn about this project, it may get rough for all of us. Xander has Malcolm's confidence, and I do not wish to threaten that. But, this is a project Devon and I have decided upon." Sanson briefly presented the reason for his visit to the PIRA veteran, concluding, "The stakes are raised by Garfield's investment in Pretemo, but perhaps it can be turned to our benefit. If rumors of Pretemo's defection are believed, perhaps the Consortium will collapse as confirmation of old suspicions shake their conspiracy. To Garfield's advantage, other cartels may react savagely to the Consortium's collusion."

Jack leaned forward. "Amos, you've always been one to see the glass half full." At Jack's movement, Lillian de Vizcaya stared and stiffened; Devon Xander shifted in his chair. Jack looked at Lillian and waved his hand. "I need to be a bit more careful, Amos, for Lillian's senses remain as efficient as ever. I wish to counsel with her before responding to your proposition. Why don't you sit with Devon, and please ask Lil to sit with me. We'll signal our decision a trice."

Amos nodded, rose from his chair, and walked over to Xander and de Vizcaya. "Jack wants to finish his breakfast with you, Lillian; Devon and I will rest here for a bit."

Lillian joined Irish Jack and spoke without preamble, "What did the watchman want?" They immediately launched an animated discussion. Though Sanson and Xander could not hear their conversation, their initial disagreement was apparent.

Jack replied, "He has a mission that requires our expertise in its planning and design. He knows we were not pleased to learn how we were used in the Nogales affair, and thought we might be interested in their response to the assassination of the Latina Border Patrol agent. He offers no compensation beyond our bare expenses while we tutor them in our arts and crafts. They will come to us for the instruction. In that way, our risk is more within our control."

"Can they be trusted?"

"Sanson's reliability is absolute; Xander is new to our business, but he is trusted by Amos. And, for a year, Devon and I shared the cause. I think we can rely on their discretion."

"Then, I will agree to the association. But, I am inclined to reservations for the time being."

"I rely on your . . . inclinations . . . Dear Lillian; they have assured our safety for a long time."

They raised and touched their cups, and Irish Jack nodded toward Amos. Amos and Devon joined them, and the four ordered more coffee and chatted for a while; then Sanson and Xander laid a few Euros on the table and departed. Kavanaugh and de Vizcaya lingered in quiet conversation.

Arturo Pretemo and Mansel Barcqe, fathers of the cartel lieutenant and the well-known journalist, had been diplomats assigned to the Mexican embassy in Washington, DC. Both were successful industrialists fully engaged in negotiations for NAFTA, so their appointments as commercial officers in the US capital were welcomed by the DC diplomatic community. Their casual acquaintance had solidified during the negotiations as their association grew both professionally and socially. It seemed natural that their sons, Joaquín and Marcello, would become close friends as they grew up in the capital of the free world. School, tennis court, chess board: Joaquín, brash and forward, and Marcello, more reticent and introspective, excelled and drove each other toward the top of the diplomatic social scale. As they advanced through university, however, they drifted in different directions, seeing each other less and less until they lost touch. For several years, their friends would ask, "Have you seen . . .?" They hadn't.

During his time at George Washington University, Joaquín Pretemo had caught the attention of Malcolm

Garfield. Pretemo was supplying a few of his friends with high quality cocaine transported from Mexico by diplomatic pouch, an arrangement unknown to his father. Garfield recognized that Pretemo was motivated by the opportunity to curry favor among the scions of members of the diplomatic community and the highest echelons of the US Congress. He was discreet and clever; Garfield admired the degree of favor he had established among contemporaries who might someday exercise considerable power in Washington and perhaps among the Mexican drug cartels. Garfield knew a promising career when he saw it, so he approached Joaquín with an offer he could not refuse: "Work for me and you may keep all the money you make and your name off the DEA charts. Someday, I'll call on you. Cross me and I'll bury you in Leavenworth, even better a choice prison in a 'friendly' country." It was the kind of high risk, high payoff that appealed to Joaquín, and a threat that he had no doubt would lead to a life not worth living. Though it had led to a few anxious moments through the years, he had not regretted his decision to accept Malcolm Garfield's offer.

Then, unexpectedly, Pretemo and Barcqe found themselves seated at the same table at a dinner honoring the arrival of a new US ambassador to Mexico City. Their friendship rekindled.

"Rosada, spend some time in Buenos Aires and with Tim Spurgin at Lawrence, research for a conference honoring the work of Jorge Luís Borges. It will be an opportunity for the university and for you to host an appreciation for Borges's work and for Latin American literature. During your absence, a colleague will watch over the shop. Also, while you are away, he will oversee a slight renovation to your store, one I promise will meet with your approval." Thus did Sanson put his plan in play.

The following day, a casually but fashionably dressed gentleman entered Rosada's shop, extended a manicured hand featuring long graceful fingers, and with a firm grasp introduced himself as Terrence McCrory. His tall, slender figure moved easily, and his ready smile was disarming; but, though his eyes sparkled, they did not smile. Soon, he had captivated Rosada with a wry wit and a melodic mix of Irish-English and Gaelic lilt. He was, as Amos had said, well versed in the history and literature of Ireland, and had with him a grand array of Irish music that soon filled the shop with delightful airs. In just a few days, McCrory established himself among Rosada's students and shop patrons as an affable substitute while she was arranging the tribute to Borges.

After Rosada departed, the shop closed for a week of renovations. When it reopened, it was even more amenable to the display of books and graphic arts, with the checkout station relocated such that a person at the station could see from the entrance to all exits. The entry and the windows had reinforced glazing, and the checkout station featured a heavily timbered half-counter. The renovations were attractive and functional.

"Amos! It's good to hear your voice."

"Good morning, Simon. I need your inestimable counsel."

"What's on your mind, old friend?"

"What do you know of Devon Xander before he joined the Army?"

"Amos, the record is sketchy . . . sealed, actually. Garfield reviewed it when vetting him for the mission in Mexico. Devon was born in Ireland and brought to southwestern Texas to escape his father's bad standing with the Brits. He had a rough upbringing, an Irish temper in a Latin community, but he flourished because of his attraction to Spanish culture and his skill with his fists. At the age of 15, he went to Belfast to visit his ailing grandmother and fell in with a group led by Jonathon Kavanaugh. When it came time to return to Texas, he was nowhere to be found. A year later, he appeared at Heathrow, boarded a plane and flew home to Texas. The rest you know."

"Thank you, Simon. Might we meet later this week in a quiet corner where you can tutor me in the subtleties of international free-trade zones, perhaps using Hong Kong and Colón as cases in point?"

"Thursday afternoon, lunch at 2 o'clock in Fredericksburg?"

"Thursday in Fredericksburg. Adiós."

"You seemed quite interested in today's topic, Amos, particularly as it applies to Latin America. Are you considering importing rare first editions by, say, Jorge Luís Borges?"

"Rumors, Simon?"

"Ah, Amos, much that passes for information today is mere rumor; but, then, much that gains the status of intelligence today is first perceived merely as rumor."

"Speak to me of rumors, Simon."

"Some believe Pretemo is heir apparent, next in line to head the Consortium. The Sonoran is ill—terminally, our own medical people advise—and we fully expect Pretemo's ascension after a stormy transition. Garfield believes he owns Pretemo and owning the man at the top is a prize not to be squandered. If rumor becomes information and information becomes fact, you may never work again, or you may be sacrificed to secure another perch within the Consortium leadership. Please understand that I cannot be linked with this . . . rumor—too much at stake, professionally and personally. I appreciate your devotion, but . . . well, risk management; you know how that goes. Please open your minds to alternatives, if not in objective, at least in timing. If Pretemo succeeds, Garfield thinks the whole industry will be vulnerable. The future holds endless opportunity, and your objective might succeed as a collateral or unexpected outcome sometime in one of those futures. Patience, old friend. Vengeance is a meal best served cold . . . or so it is rumored."

"It was precise, surgical the Americans might say, aimed not at us but, rather, at our operational capability. Why: To cripple us? To set in motion a succession that would identify our best and brightest as we promote within our organizations? But why is Pretemo the last man standing? Did the assassins miss him or had they a more sinister motive? Did they leave him in place because he is more valuable to them alive than dead? Who could have accomplished these attacks: The United States? Definitely. The Brits? Probably.

Others? Perhaps . . . but most likely the US.

"As for Joaquín Pretemo: Rumors of his involvement with the authorities persist; and, while he continues to contribute to our bottom line, I have an able replacement. We have total access to the police reports concerning the assassinations of your operations officers. I believe we can eliminate Pretemo in such a way that it will be interpreted simply as part of the previous operation. So, with your approval, I will manage this risk."

"How will it be seen by the public?"

"The news will be handed to a journalist with good credentials, and in need of a good story."

"Barcqe?"

"A matter of such sensitivity cannot be entrusted to Barcqe. I have in mind another who is capable and anxious to restore her place among European investigative reporters. Ariana Lentz is in Mexico to interview Marcello; perhaps we can interest her in our story and gain a deeper appreciation for the various lives of Mr. Barcqe as well. Money is welcome, but regaining her professional status is foremost on her agenda. We can arrange for our European colleagues to provide an outlet for her views. Being the able investigator that she is, she will be able to glean a plausible 'truth' from the 'facts' available to her. Pretemo will become merely one more dot, and a possible threat will be eliminated."

"An interesting proposal. Let us take it up in earnest in the morning."

Marcello Barcqe was more than mildly interested in the plane descending into Mexico City's international airport. Ariana Lentz was aboard that plane, and she was coming to interview him in the wake of his immensely successful book, *Nexes*. Written more as an extensive essay than an insider exposé, the book had captured the attention of political and law enforcement officials across the globe and, surprisingly, a broad array of general readers. An interview by the well-known European investigative reporter could launch him from regional expert to global authority. Marcello wanted to make the most of this opportunity.

He had prepared extensively for the interview. He knew, for example, that Lentz had won her most prestigious awards covering the Provisional Irish Republican Army and the ascension to legitimacy of Sein Fein, and Black September, the Munich massacre, and Israel's operations Bayone, Spring of Youth, and Wrath of God. She was among the elite observers of terrorist activity during the last three decades of the 20th century. More recently, however, her career was on "pause." In encouraging her to accept the assignment, Simon Stoddard had emphasized the opportunity to return to the top. Barcqe was prepared to help her achieve that, and to boost himself in the bargain.

Amos Sanson? On a veranda overlooking a western sea, a waiter placed a glass of light red wine of local vintage near the gloved hand of a solitary gentleman gazing into the gathering dusk.

For the moment, he was in a different universe, effortlessly moving throughout the world of rare books, searching on consignment or simply to indulge his affection for the feel and smell and sight and sound of the written word. He searched through city streets, country byways, and ancient monasteries, causing no ripples. As often as occasion permitted, from sunset minus fifteen to plus forty-five, a glass of light red wine of local vintage at his gloved hand, he sat in the fading light as the sun descended through brilliant scarlets, purples, and yellows into a western sea. Some spots don't change.

And Devon Xander? At 0300 the soft light and sound of an awakened secure satellite phone whispered "My place, 191200 Instant." Xander depressed the acknowledge button, then immediately returned to a deep, restful sleep.

VI

Special to the *Euro Press Syndicate*

Lucrative Training Contracts Going to PMF Training Camps in Central America

By Marcello Barcqe and Ariana Lentz

(PANAMA CITY) In the wake of displays of military-style tactics by cartel street soldiers, authorities are investigating a private provider of security and military training somewhere in the mountains and forests of Central America. Instructed by former members of Latin American and other elite police and military special operations units, the courses offered are thought to be as sophisticated as those provided by many of the world's top-ranked SWAT and military units, including weapons, communications, and small-unit intelligence and operations. The worldwide need for private security and military forces (PS&MF) has gained legitimacy because of increasing violence and threats to property and personnel in unsettled places across the globe. Governments, non-profits, and businesses are competing for the services of the best, even as they deplore the growth of the industry. Investigators are said to be particularly interested in allegations of connections between the training camps and the illicit narcotics industries of Latin America and Southeast Asia.

TERRENCE AMBROSE MCCRORY smiled as he walked out of the dockside warehouse in the free-trade zone of Colón. He had just landed an A&E contract to renovate a small pharmaceutical plant near Bilboa, complete with research and development laboratories for level 4 biological containment and explosives. Among the extensive provisions for security were a conference area meeting the standards for sensitive compartmented information facilities and vaults designed to protect trade secrets, financial instruments and significant amounts of cash against industrial espionage and natural disasters. And he had been invited to return tomorrow to discuss development of a private military and security force training camp somewhere in Central America. The professional fees for these projects were expected to be two percent above premium for industrial design. With generous reimbursables and project administration during construction, the value of these contracts was considerable. For a firm the size of T. A. McCrory Associates, the jobs were a bit of a stretch; but with quality and time as the drivers, and costs expected to match the need, he could augment his very competent staff with specialists to guide them. It was a once-in-a-lifetime opportunity, and the risks seemed manageable.

The Consortium was pleased with the results of the meeting: acquisition of a design development firm known for its quality and discretion. With Simon Stoddard handling the international contracts and finances, the legitimacy of the projects was unassailable. Some might complain about the training camp, but the need for private security, military and intelligence services was generally accepted in economic, political and humanitarian enterprise as necessary to manage risk and ensure profitability in an increasingly confusing and violent world. The opportunities for those with vision and money were endless.

Seated comfortably across his ornate desk from Devon Xander, Simon Stoddard went straight to the point, "Devon, four countries in Central America, with the full support of the United States, want to build a joint anti-terrorism center somewhere within the four nations to train counterterrorism specialists and to plan and execute direct-action operations against drug traffickers and insurgents across the region. The center will work with both civil and military missions to interdict drug transit routes and maintain stable governments north of the canal. Canal officials are interested in cooperating with the project, but they are not ready to openly support an activity that will reinsert the United States into their internal affairs. This project has the attention of high government, military and corporate intelligence officials here and in Latin America. Malcolm wants you as the deputy director of the project, and he has convinced our authorities that you are right for the position.

"Rumors suggest that a Mexican drug consortium that relocated its executive activities to Colón's free-trade zone is also interested in a training center somewhere in the region—and this seems to lie at the heart of Garfield's concern—to prepare for paramilitary operations against national anti-drug activities in the region between Panama and the Rio Grande. We know that Terry McCrory has a contract with a legitimate firm doing business in Spain and Latin America to develop the facilities and renovate a pharmaceutical plant in northern Spain."

"I know something of McCrory's work," interjected Xander, "because of the renovations to Rosada's building."

"Interest in the government facility is expected to be straightforward and overt. Your involvement fits well with your open-source resume. The Consortium's project, however, will be part of our package. Under your cover as deputy director of our project, Malcolm wants you to locate and monitor developments related to McCrory's contract. McCrory's work is legitimate . . . Garfield has no problem with his involvement. But, Malcolm is very interested in the Consortium's facilities and who comes and goes around them.

"As usual, Simon, you set a full table."

"No doubt, Devon, but we're playing for high stakes, and we can't afford to be shortsighted."

"I'm glad you brought up the topic of 'short sight.' The scale and scope of the two projects together is too much for one person in the field. Working for Garfield is in line with my experience but getting into and out of the mountains and jungles of Central America is the kind of mission I've worked on only a couple of times with Amos. That part of the job, especially if it includes watching over the pharmaceutical plant in Spain, requires its own focus and skill set. And traveling back and forth between Central America and Spain would expose us to more airport security checks. I imagine you know where I'm going with this."

"I do, and I am prepared to go to extraordinary lengths to entice him to reengage."

"Simon, I am interested in working for Malcolm. But I want to know more before I commit to the full range of his concerns. I'm not saying that I won't take on the project without Amos to lead on the Consortium side, but I think that we should proceed cautiously. Without Amos, the risks, including the risk of failure, may be . . . well, Simon, we can't do this without him."

"At the moment, he isn't available, Devon."

"I'm not suggesting that he come back permanently, but we can't do this without him. Neither of us trusts anyone else for a mission this sensitive."

After a brief pause, Stoddard said, "All right, Devon. You go do your homework and be alert for my call. Finding Amos may take some doing."

Nodding, Xander rose, turned and left. He was excited at the prospect of working again with Amos Sanson.

Simon turned toward, and for a while stared into, his *Deus Ex Machina.*

Ariana Lentz was pleased. Her feature on Marcello Barcqe had been accepted with very little editing and was to appear in newspapers throughout Europe within days. Papers in the United States, most notably the *New York Times*, the *Washington Post* and the *Los Angeles Times*, were negotiating with the Euro Press Syndicate for rights to publish the article in their Sunday editions. Marcello had been very open on background, sharing a great deal of information about his relationships with prominent politicians, industrialists, law enforcement authorities, and high-ranking military commands. Some sources, the names of individuals and his contacts with illegal drug trafficking, for example, he withheld, but they were discussing serious collaborations that could catapult them into the first rank of international investigative journalism. Discussions leading to their continued collaboration, coupled with their separate research and experiences, had illuminated two major activities having international impact: private military force development and training, and increasingly potent narcotics, both legal and illicit. Furthermore, Central America was not only bridging between North and South America, it was becoming the crossroads among the Americas, Europe, Asia and Africa for certain lucrative enterprises. And the Free-Trade Zone of Colón was its epicenter.

Rumors circulating among Latin American journalists suggested that a "well-financed group" was pursuing political avenues in Washington to influence decisions regarding the counterterrorism / drug interdiction training center. The group was arguing for US financial aid to four Central American countries so they could purchase training through PMF contractors rather than participate in a "US financed and controlled center" in the region. Latino decision-makers preferred to control their own destinies (and keep the keys to the gates through which drugs flow into North America?). Barcqe and Lentz believed they could exploit these dramatic issues as both reporters and novelists.

Devon Xander and Rosada Ángel Jesús sat in the coffee shop inside her bookstore discussing past and future.

"I think he really wanted simply to settle down with his books. He seemed so content when his concerns revolved around searching for rare editions. I wondered at such times what kept him in the game." Rosada sat quietly for a moment, then rose to refresh her tea and Xander's coffee.

Devon waited until she returned to the conversation. "I really didn't know much about him personally. You two had your books, but he and I had only our projects. I did know him well enough to know he'd be hard to replace."

"Where do we go from here?"

"Simon suggests that I work closely with Malcolm Garfield, and that you and I continue to work together. You have solid contacts, I can work with Garfield on several fronts, and Simon may want to send us on special operations occasionally. I think that we won't recruit a new watchman, at least for now, though Simon may want us to work with someone else on special assignments."

"Our world is changing."

"Yes."

"But we can still do what we do as well as ever we could."

"Yes."

"So, what is our next step?"

After a momentary pause, Xander replied, "If it's OK with you, I'll talk with Simon about the three of us getting together. After that, we'll see."

The next day, Xander walked into the bookstore and directly to Rosada's iPod jukebox, currently featuring the alternating sounds of Irish step dancing and IRA ballads, motioning for her to follow. Barely above a whisper, he said, "We're having lunch with Simon in Charlottesville on the 24th, and *he* will be there."

Garfield was seated behind his battleship-gray steel desk in his typical civil service office in a suburb of Washington, DC, when Devon Xander entered for one of their periodic meetings to review progress in the four-countries project. Immediately, he was on his feet walking around the desk with hand extended to greet his colleague and confidant: "Devon, it's good to see you, even though your information may be no more positive than mine." Garfield was immersed in the complexities of dealing with differences and indecision among competing players within the US government and among the sovereign states "cooperatively" developing the Central American training facility, and he suspected that Xander was no less frustrated dealing with his counterparts on the isthmus. Only moments into their discussion, Garfield's expectations were borne out.

"Malcolm, not only is there no progress to report, but the mistrust and reluctance to accept our leadership on the project is pushing us further apart. Basically, their line is to cooperate with us if we finance development of their counterterrorism and drug interdiction resources but let them purchase services and resources from their own providers. They are wide open to interoperability—compatible communications, weapons and tactics, for example—but insist upon operating within their own policy and command and control systems. They appear to be adamantly against constructing an international training camp under US management, largely because, so far as I can see, they see it as an attempt to reestablish the School of the Americas; 'subservience' is the word one of my counterparts used and it was not contradicted publicly or privately. My Latino military and law enforcement friends say nothing different on- or off-duty. The line seems firm. Even if they trust you and me, they don't trust our government . . . or theirs either. Rosada thinks the mistrust is a matter of 'acquired' culture."

"I'm not surprised, Devon. Around here, the difference between supporters and opponents of the proposal is wide and increasing. The arguments flying back and forth are similar in public, and even more distressing, in private. Many of our legislators, and some in the administration and among my fellow civil servants, really don't want to risk sharing command and control. But they insist that we interdict the flow of drugs and stop foreign terrorists before they reach our borders. They want us to act south of the border, but not appear to impose it. Our intelligence is tracking money originating offshore and passing through lobbyists and international corporations, but we have nothing near evidence that will stand up in court, even if we're allowed to present it behind closed doors. Sometimes, I'd like to send something south other than surveillance satellites and unarmed drones because I think some of these south-of-the-border Dons and organizations are as much of a threat to the homeland as those targets in Asia."

Xander chuckled and interjected, "Sounds like something a tired and wired civil servant said to me some time back in Arizona."

"And I was as right then as I am now! As far back as I can remember, it's been same ol', same ol', with guys like us doing the best we can to keep our part of the world safe for democracy."

"I hear you, Malcolm. But, we're cops and soldiers; we swore the oaths. What do you want me to do?"

"Stay with it and let me know if you sense a crack in their solid front, even if it isn't much, because I can still channel information to a few of the right people. Right now, I see no change in our control of US demand for drugs. Frankly, I expect our resources to be stretched tighter, maybe to the breaking point, as states legalize marijuana and more potent drugs and prescription painkillers go mainstream. But, as someone once said, 'Don't let what you can't do get in the way of what you can do.' In the meantime, we'll try to turn some can't-dos into can-dos."

Later, in Rosada's bookstore, Xander briefed her on the meeting with Garfield. He thought he might try to contact Sanson and offer to assist Amos because his own mission was not taking much of his time. Though patient during operations in the field, Xander did not relish sitting around waiting for policy makers to make up their minds. But Rosada advised him to stay away from Amos. She would let Sanson know of Xander's offer: "If Amos wants help, he'll ask for it and suitable arrangements will be made."

Sanson carved out two operations, one in Northern Spain and another in Central America. He reasoned that movement between Latin America and Iberia would expose him to detection and not allow him to maintain constant surveillance on the training camp in Central America. He approached Kavanaugh and de Vizcaya, who agreed to keep eyes on developments at the pharmaceutical plant through their own devices and communicate within the loop maintained by Rosada Ángel Jesús, while he took on the Central America phase.

Early reports from Spain showed little more than routine renovation of a legitimate pharmaceutical works. However, Kavanaugh and de Vizcaya, with their penchant for thoroughness and special knowledge of explosives, noticed construction of heavily reinforced structures, reminiscent of research blast chambers, that received special attention by observers who appeared only at that point. Inquiries among their friends led them to the identities of three engineers who specialized in explosive blast chambers and were believed to be active in the development and testing of conventional military mines, special operations explosive devices and IEDs. The information was passed into the communications loop maintained by Rosada.

Sanson's project was different.

Before BMNT (beginning morning nautical twilight), Sanson was in position. Shrouded in a ghillie suit, he observed the main encampment of the private military/security training center deep in the mountains and jungles of Central America. He had been on station long enough to locate the central facility and some specialized training sites, and to observe training in progress. Now he was set to photograph the trainers, trainees and visitors.

The training program was mostly abbreviated basic and advanced combat courses and specialties such as explosives and communications. Training in the urban settings was more like SWAT operations. The individual activities were geared to a wide literacy range and presented professionally and competently. And, nothing appeared to be hidden from satellite or aerial surveillance.

Sanson saw nothing that was not available to militia and other groups in the rural United States. However, the quality of the training appeared to be much higher.

After verifying the camp routine and courses, he focused on the trainees in the advanced courses. He photographed staff and trainees so Garfield could try to identify them through photographic evidence in his criminal and special operations files. If the PMF camp was training soldiers for the drug trade or other illegal activities, such matches would be important.

So far, the operation appeared legitimate. But there was one facility that appeared to be kept under wraps.

Sanson observed an area of approximately an acre, a square a little more than 200 feet on each side, on which a two-level metal building stood. What was going on inside the building was a mystery, but the building's importance was suggested by the security surrounding it and the personnel moving in and out. They appeared to be among the best of the trainees and a few of those in charge.

Security around the whole training center was tight, so Sanson's observation was limited to face and behavioral recognition. No one in the camp saluted, but deference would be noted in his report. He was determined to get a closer look. He prepared to infiltrate the camp during two days of predicted torrential downpour, and then clear out of the area for a bit of rest and meetings with Xander and Irish Jack. Together they would review progress, refine plans to finish the project and rough out a report. He got his gear together and waited for the rain.

Four days later, Sanson sat comfortably on the balcony of the Meridor Café, a light red wine of local vintage near at hand, awaiting a call summoning him to a meeting with Xander, Kavanaugh, and de Vizcaya. His phone rang. He listened for a moment, said only, "yes," and turned his attention to the setting sun.

After the meeting, he would prepare a second report for Simon Stoddard's eyes only.

While Xander's team was in Spain and Central America, Marcello Barcqe and Ariana Lentz were engaged in their own investigations.

The Consortium was disintegrating. The charisma and strength of the Sonoran had kept the executives together, but pressure from within their cartels was irrepressible. For the two journalists, the collapsing Consortium was an opportunity. Their news outlets were clamoring for articles, and they planned books analyzing similarities and differences in the management and operations of drug cartels and terrorists. They had even been approached by a couple of publishers of adventure novels. Their flowering reputations, some organizational and psychological theory, a bit of political and economic speculation, and a lot of salacious detail could keep this roller coaster going for years . . . provided they did not threaten too many of the wrong people.

"Legitimacy!" Ariana's sudden exclamation broke the silence in Marcello's study. "Lamborn wrote that the primary cause for an insurgency is the perceived illegitimacy of the rulers. Insurgency from within the ranks is always bubbling just beneath the surface of the cartels, and it is repressed only by the power of the drug lords. The move of the Consortium to Colón may have looked good to the cartel top brass, but it took them too far from their troops to keep the pressure on. When their field commanders saw a chance to assume direct control, they broke ranks and took what they felt was rightfully theirs."

"So we present it as a struggle for power, a battle among tribes bunkered in their plazas?"

"If the model doesn't fit perfectly, we'll tug and tuck here and there, and offer our informed opinions and conclusions until the message is coherent and plausible. We never have all the facts anyway. We're always assembling puzzles with a few missing pieces, but the pictures can be seen even if there are gaps. And, as you say, we can fill in a lot of gaps and still stay within journalistic license . . . maybe a little poetic license if we don't stretch the facts too thin. I think the Euro Press Syndicate will go for it. Shall I float it past Joselyn Prescott?"

"Lots of 'ifs,' Ariana, but I'm betting the 'thens' will be worth it. Let's flesh it out first. I'll take a trip up north, you go to London and the Continent, check with a few friends, and get together somewhere other than here to review the prospects."

"Sounds intriguing, Marcello. I'll call you each day at 0001 GMT. If either of us thinks we should break off inquiries, we'll say something about SCUBA diving and meet at Fantasy Island two days later."

"Sounds good. Don't hesitate to bail out if you feel squeezed. Some of the toes we may tread on won't hesitate to let us know how they feel."

A few days later, Ariana and Marcello were suiting up at the gazebo on Fantasy Island. After a refreshing dive, they went to dinner, choosing a quiet corner where they could talk freely.

"Don't probe too deeply, but let us know what you think," was Marcello's generalization of talks in Washington and New York.

Ariana summarized, "The Europeans are taking a wait-and-see approach, but they will provide us with outlets for our reporting if we keep them fully informed. As a sidebar, I picked up one other interesting tidbit, a rumor circulating among London financiers that a highly respected American financial counselor—the senior partner in a Washington international law firm—may assume control of a Spanish pharmaceutical company in the closing stages of reorganization and renovation. Any such rumors in the DC circuit?"

"No, but if it becomes germane to our inquiries, I'll check it out."

Xander was first to arrive, followed momentarily by Jack Kavanaugh and Lillian de Viscaya. Jack and Lillian sat opposite each other, together mounting a 360-degree watch. At precisely sunset minus 15 minutes, or so it seemed, Amos Sanson appeared beside them. Neither Irish Jack nor Lillian had seen him approach, but they were not surprised. Four tourists they seemed, seated on the balcony of the Meridor, watching a golden sun descend into a sea of blue and yellow, orange and red. Their conversation was quiet, their accents unique, slight Southwestern drawl mixed with the lilt of Ireland, a Spanish lady's gentle punctuation, and a nondescript formality.

Xander asked each in turn for a brief synopsis of their observations and tentative conclusions. They knew the conversation was being recorded; Devon wanted no hesitations while they waited for his hurried scribbling. He wanted a free flow without interruptions. Later they would discuss, analyze and conclude. A formal after-action debriefing as a policeman and soldier might conduct.

Kavanaugh and de Viscaya were faintly amused at the formality, but they respectfully summarized the salient factors they had observed and the conclusions they had drawn.

Lillian began, "The situation in Northern Spain is progressing nicely, the facilities are nearing completion. McCrory should come out very well positioned for the future. The most serious difficulty is the ownership/management structure. Compartmentalization is extensive, suggesting that parallel legitimate and illegal operations are possible, and with what little we know about the ownership/management, at least moderately likely. We think the organizational and financial arrangements should be examined by someone able to sift through arcane and convoluted legal and financial machinations."

Irish Jack continued, "The security surrounding the project is of the highest order. Penetrating the facility and organization may not be possible without political pressure. Even then, they may be able to control the processes, industrial and political, in such a way as to delay, possibly prevent, meaningful investigation. It is apparent that the project is well financed, and money speaks fluently in many languages."

Xander turned to Amos Sanson, "Generally, the operation in Central America appears to be well managed and financed, to offer very high-quality skill-development instruction and to support the militaristic aspirations of a broad clientele. The basic trainees seemed to be self-disciplined and highly motivated. The advanced trainees were, for the most part, very competent intermediate operatives who advanced through their courses with alacrity and intelligence, achieving relatively high proficiency in skills expected of military noncommissioned and company-grade commissioned officers. Their leadership performance was, for the most part, effective, though their 'troops' were their peers and basic trainees who consistently demonstrated their willingness to be led. In a sense, they were performing in an artificial atmosphere and had much to gain by cooperating with the program, but they appeared to recognize the opportunities and to be intent upon making the most of them. The very few poor performers simply disappeared.

"I observed visitors, some in uniforms, some in civilian clothing, who were treated with respect and deference. None of the visitors stayed overnight.

"Spanish was the camp language. Visitors either spoke Spanish or interpreters were provided by camp administrators.

"Security was very good and was integrated into the training. There was little that was not open to aerial surveillance. Training took place in all types of weather and levels of visibility.

"The training is legitimate for military and security operations conducted by governmental and private military-style organizations and is of high quality."

Xander delivered the final summary report, "Positions in Washington and among my friends in Central America have changed very little. There is concern in Latin America for US interference in their national affairs. Americans want a strong hand in interdicting the flow of drugs into the US. Through NAFTA, the US has a strong hand in Mexico, but efforts to extend US trade agreements throughout Latin America are met with mixed reactions. The roots of the conflict run deep.

"In the war on drugs, the Latinos want to cooperate; they bear a heavy burden in social and paramilitary conditions. They think US and European demand is driving Latin American supply chains, and they don't see any headway being made by Americans and Europeans. The cartels take their licks and come back strong, and the people have to live with the chaos.

"They recognize and suffer with the corruption and want military and law enforcement training and technical assistance, but they don't want to return to US hegemony. They want economic cooperation, but not at the expense of what little they have.

"Latinos are skeptical of US domination in so-called cooperation, and Americans are skeptical of Latin capabilities of dealing with their internal affairs.

"I wish I had something better to say. What do you think?"

An hour after the discussion began, they had nearly completed the puzzle. A few gaps to fill, but they were generally satisfied with the information that Xander and Rosada would fashion into an executive summary for Malcolm Garfield.

Then Amos Sanson spoke with quiet authority, "Devon, deliver the first report orally, nothing in writing but displaying readiness to respond to questions. Facts when possible and opinions only when asked for. Let them come to you with direct questions. We are likely to learn more about their real interests by listening to them fill in gaps in their knowledge. If you give more, provide little or no information about your ways and means." Kavanaugh and de Viscaya nodded their concurrence.

Glancing toward the entrance to the café, Lillian said quietly to her companions, "Company." Sanson rose, then extended his left hand. "Welcome, Marcello. Ah, the ever-artful Ariana; we have not met, but your work is well known. May I presume this is not a chance encounter?"

Xander and Jack brought two chairs to the table and Amos signaled to the waiter. Irish Jack noted the delicate dimples at Lillian's mouth, a clear sign that the ever-vigilant Basque patriot was fully focused on the newcomers. She was well aware of Lentz's writings of earlier Basque and Irish troubles with Madrid and

London. Drinks were ordered and refreshed, and the six appeared to settle into friendly reunion.

Barcqe opened the conversation, "Gentlemen and lovely Lillian, we come bearing gifts to exchange without attribution for such as you might offer in return."

Xander deliberately looked at each of his three companions. Receiving their assent, he replied, "Please continue, a bit at a time if you will."

"Gracias, mi amigo. Let me know if the pace or sensitive boundaries are exceeded."

Just so, the exchange became more intimate, to be closed a while later by Marcello Barcqe, "Summarizing, we found no mysteries while plumbing the arcane depths of the organization of the projects in Spain and Central America. The records are brilliantly orchestrated to terminate at a legitimate and defensible exposition of ownership and control. But, of course, rumors abound regarding the realities and intentions of any who might be producing, directing or waiting in the wings to step into less clearly defined roles or move to center stage at the appropriate cue."

As if in afterthought, Marcello added, "Toward the close of our inquiries, a trusted friend suggested to me that two of his A-1 clients suggested to him that Ariana and I were uncomfortably close to treading on tender toes. So, I leave you, fair friends, with this conundrum: if everything were simply legitimate but complex, why would Ariana and I have been warned off?"

Irish Jack: "You do occasionally make lives a bit more difficult when you report what you know."

Lillian: "But, in doing so, you inform us and make us better at what we do because we must constantly maintain our proficiency in navigating the dancing landscape."

Sanson: "It is a game, really, played expertly by determined professionals intent upon their own best interests."

Marcello: "Amos, do you think Ariana and I are in danger?"

Sanson: "Being highly valued members of the Fourth Estate may provide less protection than a pair of Kevlar vests. We may not be fully aware of whose tentacles reach how far into our daily lives."

Marcello, turning to Ariana: "Perhaps, my dear, we should retire to a quiet place and work on our book."

Ariana, glancing around the table: "How is it that you know so much about our inquiries?"

Xander: "Thank you, Ariana and Marcello, for your stimulating contribution to our discussion."

As Ariana and Marcello took their leave, Marcello allowed Ariana to walk out of earshot, turned, and said softly to Devon, "By the way, rumor has it that Simon Stoddard intends to take an equity position, perhaps the managing interest, in the subject of your inquiries in Central America and northern Spain." He hurried to catch up with Ariana.

Sitting comfortably in the corner window of the bookstore on 4th and Main, Devon Xander updated Rosada Ángel Jesús on the discussion in Casco Viejo. As dusk gathered, they slipped into the relaxed conversation so common between close friends.

"Devon, you are leading different lives now, and they are reflected in the different voices you use when relating the reports of your colleagues: strict formality with Amos, a little less so with Simon, the jargon and banter of cops with Malcolm, a bit more guarded with Jack and Lillian, and after the business is discussed, the relaxed manner of neighbors with me."

"Rosada, sometimes I feel like I am a different person with each of you. Amos has always been formal, keeping his affairs in compartments behind a blank door, maybe because there is something in his mind that he has to keep out of the way when we are working. Simon wants to maintain control, to impress you with his expertise while wanting you to feel like his buddy. Malcolm, well, he and I are part of a close-knit fraternity; we are cops, partners walking the mean streets of society. Jack and Lillian are always a bit off to themselves, though Jack led me through some rough stuff during my coming of age. And you, Rosada, with you I am completely at ease, and you have filled in a lot of holes in my knowledge and understanding about the games we play. Simon is a player; I don't think he has lied to me, but I think he hasn't laid all his cards on the table. The rest of you have my back when I'm on the street. It's all games as Amos says, and you guys won't let me down."

"Devon, don't ever forget, not even for a moment, that these games are played in the fog on quicksand with rules made up by each player to suit his needs and the situation at hand."

"Simon, Amos and I think you may be drawn through a black hole that will leave you stranded on the other side."

Stoddard had just explained to Xander that the collapse of the Consortium had created an opportunity for an international conglomerate that he advised to acquire the pharmaceutical plant in northern Spain and the Central American PMF training facility. The PMF camp had several lucrative contracts and the support of local authorities who did not wish to fall back under the influence of the Americans, and the plant near Bilboa was coming along nicely.

"Ah, a stellar metaphor, Devon. Another universe, so to speak," mused Simon Stoddard. He paused for a moment, then continued, "However, no matter the universe, it is only business."

VII

Sunday Sentinel Book Reviews

WASHINGTON, DC — *Tomorrow, at the weekly luncheon of Washington's Chapter of the National Press Club, Marcello Barcqe, award-winning author based in Mexico City, returns to discuss his latest book, co-authored with one of Europe's top investigative reporters, Ariana Lentz,* Point–Counterpoint: The Militarization of the War on Drugs. *The book explores the growing employment of military-style combat forces by both the drug cartels and local/federal law-enforcement organizations in the escalating battle for control of the illicit drug trade in North America, and the growing threat in Europe as Latin American drug lords seek to expand their markets. Every bit as scintillating as his previous best seller,* Nexus: Cartel Cash, Terrorist Tactics, and Social Angst, *Barcqe's newest assessment, augmented by the long-time expertise of one of Europe's most experienced observers of international terrorism and its methods, adds detailed insight into the increasingly well-orchestrated violence on both sides of the law in one of the most important societal conflicts of our time.* The Sentinel *also contains a feature article with the same title.*

SIMON STODDARD SAT QUIETLY, staring into the depths of his exquisite *Deus Ex Machina*, searching for guidance as he wrestled with a decision he must make by the end of the day: should he abandon his usual roles as counselor or setting up intricate organizations to shield clients from scrutiny, to take a more active role directing the activities that in the role of attorney he would be hiding so professionally?

In representing his clients, Simon did not depend upon loopholes in the statutes; as a matter of fact, he did not believe that loopholes existed. He believed that laws simply meant what they said. He relished interpretation, argument and precedence, but he considered them to be merely an extension of the common law process. Whatever lay within those parameters was *the law*, was legal and proper, and was not to be thought of as the pejorative "loophole."

So, his hesitation was based upon management of the considerable responsibility for decisions by himself, his associates or his agents. As Devon Xander had said, he could be drawn inextricably through a black hole into the "dark side," and he was not so naïve as to believe that the business of the dark side did not differ on occasion from the side of law and order. And, he was not certain that he would be as safe and his position as secure as in his present circumstances.

So, Simon Stoddard sat quietly staring into the depths of his exquisite *Deus Ex Machina*, waiting for the message to emerge before the end of the day.

"It's done, Devon. After this project, I'm through dealing every day with myopic bureaucrats and narrow-minded politicians." Malcolm Garfield was briefing Devon Xander on his current project and Devon's role in it. "My retirement has not been announced yet, but my successor has been selected and will accompany us on our trip south of the border."

Xander left through Garfield's private back door as the arrival of his next visitors was announced. He was surprised at Garfield's coming retirement, but he was far more intrigued by Garfield's interests in the future. Xander wanted to maintain the associations that Garfield had developed and would no doubt expand when released from the bureaucracy. Amos Sanson, Jack Kavanaugh, and especially the openly skeptical Lillian de Vizcaya, would recognize the potential, but they would insist upon thoroughly examining all the liabilities, real and imagined, before they agreed to a full partnership. After all, they had operated on the dark side for a long time, and they would think hard before exposing themselves to anyone with Garfield's law-enforcement credentials and associations.

Sunlight brightened the walkway only briefly each day when the sun aligned with the narrow street bounded on both sides by three- and four-story walk-up buildings, small shops at street level and a mix of apartments and offices above. The day was cool, the soft cloth glove on his right hand did not seem out of place as the elderly gentleman peered down the narrow cobblestone street.

He was on a quest, to find the bookshop of Donald Quixote Alvaria-Iverson and examine a rare illuminated manuscript of *Don Quixote de La Mancha*. The manuscript had been, or so it was said, copied by hand by the scholarly priest-confessor to an aristocratic Castilian officer who had provided the artistic illumination and illustrations for the manuscript. The two, priest and soldier, had spent every free moment during their service to the Spanish conquerors of Mexico working on the manuscript. One of a kind, if authentic, the manuscript could be of considerable value. It had been brought to his attention by Rosada Ángel Jesús, who had learned of it during her government service in Latin America when she had sought the expertise of the professor from the Universidad de Guanajuato, and the aging Alvaria-Iverson had recognized her ken for Spanish and Latin American writers. She visited Alvaria-Iverson's shop frequently, becoming known on the street as "La Aprendiza de Don Quixote." For the moment content in "retirement," Amos Sanson was looking forward to meeting the rare-book dealer.

The delicate ring of a bell announced his entrance into the shadowy interior of the bookshop. Immediately a gentleman who looked remarkably like Miguel de Cervantes Saavedra appeared in the gloom. "Señor Sanson?" The words came softly and clearly, and with a degree of expectation that the inquiring inflection would be answered. "I have been awaiting your arrival with great interest."

"Yes, Señor Alvaria-Iverson, as have I. You have been the object of my professional curiosity since our mutual friend suggested that I visit your shop. The Castilian manuscript has interested me for some time; her suggestion was most welcome."

"Yes, the Castilian manuscript. She told me of your interest during my visit to your country for her tribute to Borges. The conference was stimulating and very well organized; it reminded me of my best days as a teacher. And, if it is not offensive to you, please address me simply as 'Don Quixote'; my friends often think I have slipped into that identity as the years have advanced."

"Very well, Don Quixote, I am honored by your friendship."

"Please, then, step into my workroom." With that, Don Quixote led Sanson through an armored door into a climate-controlled warehouse, and directly to a glass-encased "clean room" of enviable proportions. "This is my domain into which very few are admitted. You come with La Aprendiza's imprimatur and are welcome. My assistant has laid out the Castilian manuscript for your examination. We will leave you to your work. If you have need of us, press the green button by the clean-room door. You will need one of us to open the doors."

"Gracias, mi amigo. I have long anticipated this moment."

"No hay de que, Señor." Señor Alvaria-Iverson and his assistant left Sanson to visit the Castilian manuscript.

Two hours later, Sanson pressed the green button and the assistant ushered him through the waning afternoon light to Señor Alvaria-Iverson's desk near the street entrance to the bookshop. "I have concluded my examination, Don Quixote; in due course, I think I will present you with an impressive offer. Buenas tardes, Señor." With a jingle of the bell, he departed.

Ariana Lentz looked up from her computer screen and spoke to Marcello Barcqe as he entered her study in the bungalow under the trees lining the sun-drenched beach bordering their Caribbean hideaway.

"Check this, Marcello. Belgian counterterrorism just took down a Jihadist who according to verified reports was planning to assassinate or kidnap a very influential financial executive suspected of laundering drug money on the Continent. Authorities had been tipped off by someone inside a ring of narcotics importers and were able to grab the guy off the street without incident. He was a former French Foreign Legion paratrooper who was linked with the mercenary trade and known to have access to some pretty heavy weaponry, so they snatched him quickly before he could draw or run. My contact believes that the police were probably tipped because the guy was about to take out an important link in the drug-terrorism money chain. She has information from a reliable source that the drug side of the deal is linked to a consortium operated out of the free-trade zone in Colón, but she can't corroborate it. She wonders whether I can help with the Caribbean end."

"That fits well with our investigation," replied Marcello, "and the Jihadist's link with the Foreign Legion plays well into our theme of militarization of drug operations on both sides of the law. Did you receive a photograph of the guy? I think Malcolm Garfield got a lot of face-recognition imagery when he sent Devon Xander to check the PM camp in Central America. If we can put this guy in the camp, we should have corroboration for a link between the camp and terrorism.

"We do need to discuss whether your 'contact' is a source or a collaborator. I am always open to a reliable source, but taking on a partner is another matter."

"At no time in the past has she been more than a cultivated source. I have some trade goods that should satisfy our relationship without opening any questions about collaboration. Expanding Latin American drug cartel interests in EU markets and increasing radical Islamic recruitment of young Muslims in Europe provide trade topics for both terrorism and drug peddling.

"This is the second time I've gone through a wave of terrorism in Europe. Perhaps the Young Turks on all sides see opportunities in going to war. We know that some in the top echelons are perfectly willing to send the cannon fodder into battle, and rake in the spoils that litter the landscape. And the PMFs, drones and arms dealers are waiting in the wings for their fifteen minutes on stage.

"It may seem a bit gauche of me, Marcello, but the powers that be on both sides are serving up a cornucopia of food for thought and ink for our pens."

"Ariana, my love, your mix of metaphors is delightful, and unerring. In dealing with your colleague, I'll follow your lead. By the way, I have some intriguing information concerning Malcolm Garfield."

And so, their conversation continued down this new and as yet uncirculated path.

Devon Xander, once again in the comfortable familiarity of Rosada Ángel Jesús's coffee shop, continued with his conclusions from his last meeting with Malcolm Garfield.

"Malcolm is still a cop, Rosada. I think he'll have a tougher time adapting than I had. I was a border cop, up to my neck in the low life of cross-border affairs, and

I had a deep involvement in one stage of the Irish Troubles. Up from the streets is not the same as in from the Georgetown brownstones. And, I saw stuff in Kosovo that chilled me to the bone. Excepting a few short-term investigations, Malcolm hasn't lived at my level on the street. And I am not sure all the people we deal with will appreciate associating with a former federal cop. I still get an occasional cold shoulder because I'm a gringo cop.

"In a couple of days, Amos, Simon, and I are getting together to talk about Malcolm. I intend to ask about rumors that someone who looks a lot like Simon is getting directly involved in some of the programs we have been involved in and whether having two cops on the payroll is in Simon's best interests, particularly since Malcolm and I still have more than just a little bit of "cop" in us. Amos and Simon have been operating in the fog for so long that right and wrong don't always come into the picture; Malcolm and I may not be there yet."

"And," replied Rosada, "Amos has been going through his own personal reassessments. Not too long ago, he seemed to be on his way out but he came back in. The times, they are a-changin'."

"The term used recently to describe the interregional conflagration among cartels is 'Balkanization.' Our Consortium is consumed in the flames spreading across Mexico." So began The Sinaloan as he opened an emergency meeting of the three-cartel drug Consortium in its warehouse in the Colón free-trade zone in Panama.

"The experiment is over. Our ability to cooperate cannot be sustained because we have dissension within our families. Our own policies aimed at strengthening the paramilitary capabilities of our street soldiers have contributed substantially to the disintegration. They are stronger and we are weaker for it. The United States has increased its efforts to interdict through cooperation with national authorities in Latin America. The drones that threaten terrorist leaders in Asia and Africa are as close to us as to them. Graft and corruption remain in our arsenal, but they appear to be weaker in the face of American pressure in its war with us. We must look after our own interests. I intend to continue my relationship and financial support for the projects in Central America and Spain. I say this to you as a mark of my respect and the good faith we have maintained among us during the period of our cooperation. The experiment has run its course. Another time, perhaps."

Choosing not to look The Sinaloan in the eyes, the other two gentlemen nodded assent.

With that, the only man to speak during the brief conference was instantly surrounded by his bodyguards and walked briskly out of the room.

Simon Stoddard was pleased.

His plan for taking control of the Consortium's investments in Central America and Spain was proceeding just as he had designed. The group of PMF CEOs he had formed was not just interested but had fully subscribed to the acquisition price. He retained the role of chief counsel, the role he coveted most. In it, he could guide development of the enterprise while retaining the lawyer–client relationship. He had the power, provided he could hold their trust. Some of them were additions to his stable of clients, but they were linked organizationally, and especially financially, to his more established clientele. Stoddard was confident that the principal investors would keep tight reins on the new members.

To establish the reality of control, he had cultivated his position with that inner circle of principals and had structured the organization accordingly. The executive board was his client, and the associations among its members were characterized by their passage through attorneys who could protect themselves and their clients through attorney–client privilege—links that could be severed selectively should the need arise. The outer ring of board members and investors was more exposed, but they were no less distanced from the inner board and themselves than were the inner Board from each other.

Financial arrangements were arcane. Stoddard knew that old rules of international finance were changing, and that several countries could (and likely would) meander covertly through the dark side of cyberspace. So, he established the organization and investments within defensible bounds. The finance and organization could be discerned, but only after brutally difficult and expensive investigations after which authorities (or anyone else with the power and reach) would discover that everything met the letter of the law. Simon Stoddard was master of his domain and confidant in his belief in no loopholes.

Professionally and ethically, he was satisfied that the facilities in Central America and Spain could be owned and operated legitimately, and their legitimacy defended legally. Financially, they were expected to operate at a profit sufficient to retain the interest of the outer circle of investors (perhaps requiring an occasional bit of convincing to remain content with their ROI) but not at a rate of return generally sought by the inner circle. The members of the executive board expected to profit along with the other investors, and to promote various interests in various ways within their own risk-management strategies. Stoddard's design was such that an occasional rotten limb could be pruned without damage to the tree.

Simon Stoddard was very pleased.

"A new dimension has been added to the debates over American imperialism," began Marcello Barcqe as he opened the discussion with Ariana Lentz. "Don Quixote Alvaria-Iverson, an aging scholar from the university in Guanajuato, has emerged as the 'intellectual' most quoted by opponents of greater US involvement in internal anti-drug and anti-terrorism activities in Latin America in general, and Mexico and Central America in particular. An expert in the history of the Spanish and US presence in Latin America, he years ago described US interests as exploitation, though 'Yankee imperialism' is usually the way it comes out in arguments from coffeehouses in the plazas to capitals throughout the region. I have found no record of current involvement in anti-American activities and he refuses to comment on the influence of his earlier works. I'm certain, however, that we can use this together with the thoughts of other 'intellectuals' to add depth and substance to *Point–Counterpoint*."

Ariana replied, "That's great news, Marcello. European and Middle Eastern thinkers have written a lot of philosophical stuff to justify their actions and spread their ideas. Adding respected commentaries by Latin Americans punctuates the worldwide nature of drug trafficking, terrorism, and security contractors. We can do a chapter that will go a long way toward making our book more than just a passing fancy on the *New York Times* best-seller list.

"My contacts in London are all abuzz over rumors of the collapse of the Colón drug Consortium. Have you picked up any information about that in DC or Mexico City? A related topic they couple with news of the disintegration of 'the great experiment,' is how it might affect a pending deal for acquisition of the PMF training camp and the pharmaceutical plant near Bilboa. Josalyn is pushing hard for current information and a feature article. I can put her off a bit for a feature, but she wants to scoop the competition and is offering full byline recognition in addition to EPS cash for up-to-date reporting as the drama unfolds. This is a great opportunity to penetrate EU news markets, Marcello. Can we put something in her hands soon?"

"I've got a piece on my desktop now. By tomorrow morning, early, you should have a solid draft. It will include news and a brief commentary concerning the upcoming conference that—and this is confidential for the moment—will be Malcolm Garfield's last. His retirement will not be announced until the delegation returns to Washington after the conference. Off the record, though, 'unidentified sources,' are not confused about it. They just don't want to undermine his authority at the negotiation table.

"I'm going to Nogales for a day or so. Something significant is going down, Ariana. I think patience on our part will be rewarded handsomely."

Amos Sanson had been on station for some time, becoming an intimate part of the landscape. In addition to checking the meeting locations, hotels and routes, he was watching for the pre-op reconnaissance that would be performed by folks who might be planning an attack on Malcolm Garfield's team during the four-country discussions centering on the potential downsides of the private military and security training camp. Garfield was focused on militarization of drug cartels and law enforcement operations and the importance of Central America as a transshipment point for drugs moving into North America and Europe. Others in the US delegation would be looking into whether trainees were part of terrorist or counterterrorism organizations in Latin America.

Sanson had already reported the presence of other countersurveillance teams who he thought were probably detected by cartel and terrorist pre-op scouts and had provided surveys of routes in and around the places he was instructed to check. Guanajuato is a beautiful mix of old and new that tourists and residents love, but security teams can find daunting. And security teams seemed to be everywhere.

Among the personas Sanson presented to the residents of the city was one he affected with a disguise that was not difficult to maintain, that of "dealer in rare books, maps and manuscripts." One of his interests in this operation was Don Quixote Alvaria-Iverson, newly emerged luminary in arguments regarding American hegemony over Mexico and Central America, and possessor of the Castilian manuscript. Sanson's visits to the bookshop tucked away among the narrow streets were conducted as attempts by a secretive bookdealer to communicate with the *caballero perfecto* who dealt in rare books. In this way he accomplished two tasks: negotiations to purchase the manuscript, and back-checking to detect any surveillance that might suggest someone had detected his mission to protect the US delegation to the PMF talks. All was business in the Great Games.

"Buenos días, Don Quixote."

"Señor Sanson, welcome. It is good to see you again. No matter the outcome of our negotiations, I do enjoy our visits."

"Have you reached a decision, mi amigo?"

"Direct, as usual. I have, and I am afraid that it will disappoint you but hopefully not interfere with our friendship."

"Then you have decided against the exchange."

"Rather, I have decided in favor of a different exchange."

"And . . ."

". . . to present the Castilian manuscript to the National Museum in Mexico City, to become a permanent part of the heritage of our great republic."

"I am authorized to increase the offer substantially."

"I suppose I have my price, as do most of us, but I think I am content with my decision. Por favor, let us close the matter and take up other issues over lunch and a bit of wine."

"As you wish, mi amigo."

The two gentlemen walked slowly—the older man speaking quietly but animatedly, the younger man, hands clasped behind his back, occasionally nodding or shaking his head—to a small cantina a few doors away, where they occupied a table outside, eating polla a la parrilla and queso, and sipping a light red wine of local vintage. Late in the afternoon they rose, shook hands and parted, Don Quixote to his shop, Señor Sanson to post a report through Rosada Ángel Jesús to Xander, who would, if he thought it appropriate, inform Malcolm Garfield of its contents.

It had been an enjoyable afternoon, and a successful foray into the dancing landscape.

Devon Xander read Sanson's message for the third time. Without a doubt, Alvaria-Iverson was a force to be dealt with. Don Quixote was a true scholar; his writings were steeped in detail, scrupulously documented, and certain to be used authoritatively to question the motives of Los Estados Unidos in any dealings with Latin America. Though historical rather than current, their veracity was unassailable. They could be used by both US negotiators and their opponents in fashioning strategies and contingency plans. Xander sanitized the message and forwarded it to Garfield.

Then he sent word to Sanson, informing him of the US delegation's travel plans and meeting agendas. He included his assessment of Alvaria-Iverson's growing importance, as both a voice for both sides and a candidate for martyrdom. The aging scholar's extant writings already were part of the growing opposition to cooperation with the United States, and he refused to enter into a more active role. In Xander's estimation, Don Quixote was totally unaware that he might be more valuable dead than alive.

When she transmitted Xander's message to Sanson, Rosada could not restrain her impulse to ask Amos to look out for her mentor and dear friend. Sanson had come to that conclusion himself when he noticed that the old academic was being watched by people who might harm him in such a way that local investigators would point toward Washington. And he knew that assassination would not be necessary, a well-executed assault would be sufficient. The watchers he saw were efficient and cruel, and their handlers were coldly rational. The labored breathing of a semi-conscious old man in a hospital bed could be a graphic feature in the daily news for a long time.

In this game, there were no rules to protect the players.

Barcqe began the meeting with a resume of his time in Washington, Nogales and Mexico City. Summarizing his broad array of information under general headings, he listed several particulars, including violence in Mexico attributed to struggles for political control between drug cartels and political reformers, prescription drug overdoses among Americans, especially among upwardly mobile women, and employment of UAVs to kill terrorist leaders living in civilian neighborhoods abroad. He was toying with the notion that a lot of people north of the border were beginning to think that US leaders were stretching their authority at home and pushing the bounds of sovereignty overseas.

"That the US might employ drones and cruise missiles against the cartels in Mexico is discussed behind closed doors and on the cocktail circuit in Washington and state capitals from California to Texas. Ports along the Pacific, Gulf and Atlantic coasts are on everyone's list of critical concerns. Some have thought it fortunate that the economic downturn has slowed growth in the number of cargo ships entering our ports, perhaps buying a bit of time to prepare for the future. But, no one wants to talk about 'The New Panamax,' new free-trade zones and all that goes along with the expected increase in shipping across the isthmus.

"Of particular interest to me was an item in the Southern Poverty Law Center's Spring 2013 Intelligence Report indicating resurgence of 'conspiracy-minded patriot groups' and hate groups during the last dozen or so years. These folks just might be persons of interest for my final note regarding the PMF training facility but no one would say more than, 'It is rumored that . . .'"

Ariana followed with a summary of her travels to London and Madrid. Her sources included leading economists and business executives, and mid-level government civil servants, in addition to Joselyn Prescott and her editorial board. From them she gleaned information about the increasing flow of illegal narcotics into Europe, money laundering through American and EU banks, and fears that apparently legitimate pharmaceutical plants in EU countries, crippled economically during the recent economic downturn, intended stunning increases in the production of prescription opioids for domestic consumption and export. News of the increase in overdose deaths among US women was disturbing to Europeans because women were rising through the ranks of business and government and discontented Islamic conservatives might be sorely tempted to provide Western women with self-destructive narcotics.

She had also talked in strictest confidence with Terry McCrory about the pharmaceutical plant near Bilboa. Ariana learned a couple of things she thought added to Marcello's report about the PMF and pharmaceutical operations: Isolated, explosion-proof facilities developed surreptitiously at the plant were already online, and an unidentified but highly respected engineering scientist who had recently emerged from an extended sabbatical somewhere in northeastern Africa would head the facility and direct the R&D activities in it. He was considered an expert on IEDs, triggers and miniaturization, and had brought with him military veterans having extensive field experience with mines and EOD. If that weren't enough, extensive production of prescription opioids had been added to the architectural program. The addition did not seem to be a surprise for the owner's representatives, who were fully prepared to cover the additional costs for A&E and construction. Given the current news, McCrory was concerned, but additions were not uncommon in complex plants, the professional opportunity was gratifying, and the money was coming in with unerring fidelity. McCrory's account was corroborated by banking and public records. And, like Marcello, Ariana had heard vague rumors among business leaders about Simon Stoddard, the Bilboa plant and the four-country project in Central America.

Marcello suggested that if they could strengthen the plausible links among business interests, drug cartels and international terrorism, the new book would easily launch from the elevated platform built by his previous book and bolster their positions among the leading investigative journalists worldwide. Access to the highest levels of wealth and power would surely follow.

Ariana Lentz could hardly contain the rush coursing through her at the thought that she was returning to the pinnacle of her profession, and the power that had eluded her in the past.

Rosada Ángel Jesús was describing for Devon Xander her hybrid program for investigating associations among disparate people: "When Jack Kavanaugh and Lillian de Viscaya escaped following the episode at Nogales, there was some suspicion regarding a couple on a cruise ship shore excursion in Puerto Vallarta. I found travel records for two couples who were very close in appearance to Irish Jack and Lillian, indicating that both couples were in Puerto Vallarta during the same few days. One of the couples was a pair of attorneys on a state drug task force in the office of the attorney general of Arizona. Using those identities, I constructed unique trees for each, and the male of the couple was networked with The Sinaloan, czar of the Mexican drug cartel across the border from Nogales."

Xander suddenly leaned forward and spoke as if to himself, "Sinaloa . . . Nogales . . . the Colón Consortium . . ."

"And," continued Rosada, "Davis Thurston, deputy attorney general and director of the state drug task force for the State of Arizona, and the man chosen to succeed Malcolm Garfield."

"Can you prove it?"

"Devon, I am confident that the information is actionable, but it is not legal proof. I am in the information business, not in the business of proving guilt beyond a reasonable doubt in court. The analytical methodology is sound, and the data input is well and confidentially sourced. I judge it to be perhaps highly likely and good enough to send to Malcolm and Amos. Malcolm probably will be skeptical; Amos will know what to do with the information."

Devon Xander sat quietly for a moment, then said emphatically, "This has to go to Malcolm and Amos immediately, Rosada. Malcolm must be on guard, and if he has said anything to Thurston about Amos, Amos may be in great danger. I'm going to Washington immediately rather than on our timetable for the discussions in Mexico. Tell Malcolm that I'm coming early with important information so don't sign the retirement papers and tell him not to tell Thurston that I'm coming or say anything about Amos. Send everything to Amos and tell him to be extra careful. And, Amos may want to talk with Jack and Lillian about their exit plan for the Nogales op."

Xander paused as he reached the door, turned and said quietly, "This is a game changer, Rosada. If Thurston isn't on our side, I need to convince the right people that he can't be trusted and must be eased out or buried in the mushroom patch."

Before Xander reached Washington, Rosada informed him that Lillian de Viscaya recognized the picture of Garfield's replacement as a lawyer from Arizona who had collaborated in their passage following the affair in Nogales. Xander was confident that the identification of Davis Thurston and the association with The Sinaloan were genuine. But, he was not as confident that the information would be received well in Washington.

Malcolm Garfield met Xander at a fast-food restaurant near Xander's hotel in Arlington. Garfield listened with growing impatience as Xander made the case against Davis Thurston. Interrupting Xander in mid-sentence, Garfield said angrily, "I don't care where you got your information. I've known Davis Thurston for years. We've shared our files with his task force, and the Arizona AG's office has cooperated fully. Together, we've busted transits all along the border . . ."

"How big were the busts, Malcolm? How many shipments crossed the border without incident? The cartels lose tens of millions of dollars in cash and product annually, but they don't seem to skip a beat. Even with our success in the Nogales crossing, a lot of product ended up on the streets in America. The cartels consider such losses to be expenses against the profits, and they don't skip a beat. And the stakes are going up. They are tougher and more professional in their boardrooms and on the streets. They are buying special ops people all along the pipelines. As soon as we cut them down, they grow back bigger and meaner and more sophisticated than before. We can't stifle the demand, and we don't appear to be making headway against the corruption. They're like penicillin; we accomplish just enough to prime their pumps, and they come back stronger than before. We legalize addictions by putting more and more powerful drugs on the market, and we can't keep the duds from selling illicit prescriptions or bribing crooked cops and doctors and God knows who else on both sides of every border along every pipeline in this totally horizontally and vertically integrated global industry. Yes, you get some of them, sometimes even a lot of them. Their accountants mark it down to business expenses in lieu of local, state and federal taxes.

"Malcolm, how much of your operating budget do you get from drug busts? How many cars and boats and planes and houses do you confiscate and turn into cash to finance your operations? Without them, the politicians would be robbing your budget to finance whatever sweetheart project will keep them re-elected. It's a symbiotic relationship that keeps people in business and voters at the ballot box. Why are we spending so much to keep track of the four-country PMF school and the pharmaceutical plant in Bilboa? Both are legitimate businesses; but, we know they have a very profitable dark side.

"I may be a simple beat cop, but I've been up to my eyeballs in the Balkans, Iraq and Afghanistan, and border towns from the Sea of Cortez to the Gulf of Mexico. I've lost people on the streets and in the countrysides of three continents. I've seen the grunts take the beatings while the white-tie-and-tails crowd toast themselves with champagne. Whether it's in the cartels or the boardrooms or the legislatures' hallowed halls, crooks are crooks. *In my professional and personal opinions, Davis Thurston is a crook."*

Devon Xander paused, then continued quietly, "If you still want me on this operation, I'll stick with you. But, I'll be watching Thurston like a hawk, and if he gets out of line, I won't look around for an OK from some political wonk, I'll do what hawks do best: I'll take him out faster than a redtail snatches a barn rat."

"Jesus H. Christ, Devon, I want you there! If Thurston is what you think, you'll have to keep an eye on him. I'll be up to my eyeballs with the negotiations. If he is what you say, I've missed it all the time I've been working with him, and I might miss it again. This conference is damned important, and this job is important too. But, Devon, if you make a move on Thurston, you damn well better be more sure than you've ever been in your whole life, because *professionally and personally,* I'm all in on this one. OK?"

"OK, compadre, but you watch your 360, 24/7, and don't get too far away from the cavalry."

"Roger that, mi amigo," replied Malcolm, "now listen up. Martín Santos and I are the principals in this conversation. Whatever we decide will go into the report with recommendations to our policy folks. The main topics are, first, the increasing flow of drugs from the Far East, how that impacts the volume of traffic through Central America and Africa into North America and Europe, and, as always, where is the money coming from and going. The pharm plant in Bilboa will be part of that discussion because prescription drugs are a growing problem, and the plant could be an important link in the money path.

"Second, the PMF training camp in Central America. Lots of faces identified during the earlier project are showing up at various points in the food chain on both sides of the streets. We've got to sort out who are the good guys so we can bang on the bad guys, and watch for the turncoats. Between us, Martín and I have pretty good information, so we should be able to put our fingers on the bad guys. To do that, though, we will have to put some details on the table.

"That's where your eyes on Davis Thurston come in. He will be included in my talks with Martín, so he will be privy to our deepest secrets and, possibly, their sources. If he is who you think he is, we'll have to deal with a serious chink in our armor before the information gets outside our little circle. Dealing with it probably won't be our responsibility, but we'll have to make the case for it. Davis likes to toss his weight around. I hate to load you down with keeping track of him. You'll have plenty to do without that additional burden. But, you brought it up, so you handle it . . . any way you want. OK?"

"Yes. Do I have a bit of loose change to put to it?"

"I think the 'petty cash' pot will cover it; but let me know when you plan to drop a sizable bundle.

"Finally, and this is just between us, I'm looking for links between the cartels and Mideast terrorists. Terrorists are always looking for cash, and cartels have lots of it. And, terrorists can muddy the waters anywhere at any time. With just a little effort, they can divert a lot of our resources. Drugs on the streets have become everyday activities; a terror pop can spin everything out of control in an instant. The media, our politicians, almost everyone goes off the deep end when terror-ism is involved, actually or hypothetically. Santos and I agree on the level of the threat, but our higher-ups don't want to deal with it. They seem to think that ignoring it means it isn't there."

"The pharm plant," said Devon. "I want someone to keep tabs on their R&D. That might be the pin tying the cartels to some terrorist groups. Our current infor-mation leads me to think they are working on small high-impact devices that can be deployed easily, justi-fied in the legitimate arms trade, especially for covert activities, and marketed anywhere cash is available. Stuff like that means you don't have to drone-dive a city block to swat a fly; the PR value alone is worth the effort. If they work up something that absolutely defies detection, we'll all be behind the eight ball. They'll have all the time and money they need to work on it, and they won't have to try to hide it in some government budget. The pharm plant and PMFs, Malcolm, both are aboveboard and can keep legitimate deep, dark secrets, and both have access to more money than any govern-ment or corporation can hide from political hacks or the tax man."

"I don't disagree, Devon, but you hit the biggest obstacle to watching them when you point out that they are legitimate businesses. I'll do what I can, but at some point Homeland Security, maybe even State or Justice or Commerce, will need to be brought in, if for no other reason than the cost of the surveillance. It's more than we can handle, financially and politically. Those of us in the stovepipes can only do so much; per-sonal chits don't cover this much cooperation."

"It's hell being working stiffs in the soot and heat."

"You got that right. I'll see you in Guanajuato."

Guanajuato: The pleasantries had hardly got under way when Davis Thurston broke in to announce that the conference should get on to the business at hand, that polite palaver was not getting to the agenda driving the conference, and that while Malcolm Garfield was leading the charge for America, he was directing the charge. No one seemed surprised; Thurston needed no introduction among those dealing with the drug traffic along the border between California and New Mexico.

Thurston was the current leader of an influential clan that had emigrated to the American West from England in the mid-19th century. These second sons who had helped build the great cattle baronies that dominated the vast Western open ranges were part of the lore and legend of cowboys and vaqueros that still captivates young and old alike. Thurston's branch of the family tree had switched from cattle range to courtroom as water rights came to dominate the legal landscape of the Southwest. Davis Thurston had gravitated toward public service, making his mark in negotiations with Mexico over use of the waters of the Colorado River. His experience in dealing across the international border provided a platform for his selection to join, and eventually head, the Arizona attorney general's drug task force. Intelligent and politically savvy, Thurston was well-connected in Phoenix, Washington and Mexico City, and appeared to be the perfect choice to replace Malcolm Garfield.

However, Martín Santos did not share the opinions of the USDEA leadership regarding Davis Thurston. Santos also had people who understood the narcotics trade along the border with the United States, and they were clearly concerned about opening their intelligence and operations to an American delegation that included Thurston.

Xander quickly picked up on the Mexican reluctance to deal with Davis Thurston. After talking with Amos Sanson, he decided to share his concerns with Santos. Talking with Santos without informing Malcolm Garfield was a bit unnerving. For an American to take such a step could be interpreted as disloyalty, even treason, by those engaged in the war on drugs.

Martín Santos listened attentively, asking occasional questions but making no statements of his own. When Xander finished, both men sat quietly for several minutes. Santos broke the silence: "I must treat this as important intelligence, and hand it over to my people. I will classify it possibly true, from a reliable source. Thank you, Devon; I know how difficult this is for you. We must have solid evidence, but I trust your assessments. We will watch Davis Thurston very closely; your people may notice our heightened interest. Thank you for your trust, and your friendship."

They stood, shook hands and walked in opposite directions. As soon as Xander was out of earshot, Martín Santos spoke into his encrypted phone to his DDI. "Meet me now. We've got a rather large fish to fry."

Without a ripple, Amos Sanson retreated from the scene.

Three days later, the bilateral Guanajuato Conference closed with little fanfare. The principals hoped to return to their capitals with detailed confidential reports that would guide policy decisions in both Washington and Mexico City. However, while passing through the Guanajuato airport to board a plane for Phoenix, Arizona, Davis Thurston paused for an impromptu interview with the press during which he praised Martín Santos as "the heart and soul of the agreements reached during the conference, agreements that will lead to sweeping actions against the drug cartels on a number of fronts." Without Santos, effective action to curb the cartels would be impossible, claimed Thurston.

Regularly monitoring discussions among the old grandfathers idling away their days in the plazas and cantinas, Amos Sanson overheard many details of the conference. He heard, for example, that the head of the US delegation was often contradicted, and privately belittled, by the man said to be his successor, and that Thurston clashed openly with Martín Santos during the meetings. Among the speculation Sanson overheard were rumors that the cartels intended to assassinate Santos soon after the conference adjourned. The old grandfathers said that Thurston's statements during the conference, and particularly the airport interview, were clear signals to the cartels that Santos was to lead the crackdown but that Thurston would challenge that assignment in Washington, and failing that, would try to limit US appropriations for the crackdown. Sanson reported all of these observations, carefully noting the sources claimed by the old men, and finished his report with his opinion that the information should be checked carefully because the people in the plazas and cantinas were just as likely to get it right as to get it wrong.

The day after the Guanajuato Conference closed, Martín Santos was found in his office, dead from a single gunshot to the head, the bullet passing from the left side of his brain to the right, his service pistol tightly clenched in his left hand, his watch undisturbed on his left wrist. Santos was known to be equally proficient with firearms with both hands, but his close associates knew that his periodic pistol qualification schedule was always shot with his right hand. Not long after, Davis Thurston returned to the private practice of law in Phoenix, Arizona. Nothing more was heard about Malcolm Garfield's retirement.

Seated at the book-strewn coffee table in the corner window of the bookstore, coffee and teacups on the table between them, Devon Xander finished telling Rosada about the funeral.

"It was a quiet, private service on a gentle slope up to a western ridge. The sun was about to set when I thought I saw someone standing by a tombstone on the ridge, but the sun was in my eyes so I wasn't sure. My attention refocused on the ceremony as it ended and the sun set behind the ridge. When I looked back up at that spot on the ridge, no one was there. After the service, Malcolm and I walked up to the tombstone on the ridge and turned to look back at the funeral site, and I thought, 'a perfect perch for watching the funeral and everything going on for two or three hundred yards around the grave site.' I'm beginning to think like him, find a place where I can see everything and have the sun at my back."

Rosada spoke softly, "From time to time, he retires from the field, rests on the sideline for a bit, then returns for another joust. His rests appear to be lasting a little longer these days . . . rare books seem to be occupying his time a little longer than before."

Night overtook the sun in the small mid-American city as Devon and Rosada talked quietly and sipped occasionally from brightly colored paper cups, content with their company and their personal thoughts.

Amos Sanson sat quietly in the softening light of the disappearing sun, a glass of light red wine of local vintage in his left hand. He very much liked Devon Xander and Rosada Ángel Jesús, and the idea of liking someone troubled him, and he was not sure why. Recurring thoughts of his childhood friends left him strangely melancholy, looking to the solitude of books, yet remembering the presence of friends whose lives were not threatened, or lost, by their relationship to him. Professional associates all knew and weighed the risks for themselves, but for friends, he felt personally responsible for their lack of awareness. More and more he thought of being out, but where and to what? Books satisfied him but exposed him to the demons of the light while he dealt in that vocation. The darkness provided protection, but in the darkness, there also lurked demons. And the brief moments of twilight were so . . . well . . . brief.

Sanson decided to speak directly to Simon about Devon Xander. That Xander had become a useful and dependable asset was clear, but Amos thought Xander not to be so well suited to the dark side. Though he had spent time during his youth with Jack Kavanaugh and the PIRA, he had opted for law enforcement as both soldier and civilian; he had become a dedicated lawman. Serve and protect: in that role he excelled, and in that role, he had served and protected Sanson well. His brief foray into assassination had been carried out with skill and courage, but the circumstances were singular, and exceptional. The hurt visited upon Rosada Ángel Jesús had fueled Xander's desire but not his appetite for murder. That Xander could kill when the occasion demanded was not in question, but while his mind could engage in the transaction, his conscience seemed less open-ended. *Serve and protect*: that placed Xander more at the side of Malcolm Garfield, where he had done well and was positioned to do more. With Garfield returned to his role and authority in the DEA, Xander would be sought to extend Garfield's reach into, and perhaps a step or two beyond, the twilight. There, Xander would cement Stoddard's legitimacy with Garfield and a number of "authorized agencies" of industry and government.

Sanson would remain in Simon's employ, but his assignments would reflect a more graceful pace of observations, and the inexorable march of time. Sanson (and others) on one side, Garfield and Xander (and others) on the other, and Stoddard bridging the in-between: a dancing landscape in which only those comfortable amidst chaos could hope to survive.

VIII

FOOTSTEPS ALONG THE WAY

TWENTY-FIVE YEARS LATER, on the occasion of their thirty-fifth high school reunion, Jan sat alone with four spirits at their usual table in Yankee's. She looked up, then stood up and rushed toward the door, words and tears flowing uncontrollably.

Jan: John Paul! Is it you? Is it really you? You're here! You're here!

John Paul: Hi, Jan. Where is everyone?

Jan: Oh . . . you don't know.

John Paul: Know what?

John Paul and Jan moved to their places at the table, sat down and continued their conversation.

Jan: They're gone.

John Paul: Gone?

Jan: All dead.

John Paul: Dead? All dead?

Jan: All.

John Paul: How? What happened?

Jan: Brad was killed in the war. Mandy couldn't get

on without him. Suzanne and Wil died in a car crash on the bypass. All, gone.

John Paul: When?

Jan: It seems so long ago. Brad was a medic in the war and was awarded the Silver Star for saving lots of wounded soldiers. He hated the killing and the dying, but he felt he should do his duty, should share their dangers and fears. And he would not protect himself. He kept going back into battle, time after time, to try to save all those poor, hurt boys. It broke Mandy's heart. She seemed to get through it. She finished nursing school and was doing well at City Hospital . . . but after a while, she gave up. She couldn't forget him, so she just gave up. Suzanne and Wil, they went to State Teachers College, came home to teach in our old high school, and fell even more in love. If they had to go, it's good that they went together. How in the world would either of them ever have got along without the other? They grew up no more than next-door neighbors apart, and after they married, they did not ever spend a night apart. Funny how some old clichés seem to fit some people perfectly. How many lives do you think they enriched as teachers, coach and principal?

John Paul: I didn't know. I didn't know. But you're here.

Jan: As I always have been. And now, you're here. Where have you been? What have you been doing? It's been so long, but it seems . . . now . . . like only yesterday, like when we were all together at the end of that summer so long ago. Tell me, tell me everything, where you've been, what you've been doing . . . why you never came back, "to join here whene'er we can to tell not less

than all the truths, nor more, and renew abiding love."
We always wondered. I was so afraid to come here
today . . . so certain, and afraid, that I would be alone.
And then you appeared.

John Paul: And you? How have you spent the years?
Married? Children? Career? You always said that someday you would be a lawyer or a CEO. You were the
smartest one of us; without you, Brad and I wouldn't
have made it through Algebra 2. You look so good . . .

John Paul's cell phone rang, interrupting him in
midsentence. He tried to ignore it, but it rang again
and again.

John Paul: I've got to take this or they'll just keep
calling. Excuse me for a moment.

John Paul rose and walked away. When he returned,
he sat down and took her left hand in his gloved right
one. The glove was soft cloth the color of his blazer.
Jan's eyes lingered on the glove.

John Paul: I've got to go.

Jan: But . . .

Softly, John Paul interrupted her: I've got to go.

Jan: Please, don't go. I have so much to tell you.

John Paul: I must . . . meet me; meet me here on this
date in two months' time. I promise to tell you everything and to listen for as long as you want. Will you . . .
will you come?

Jan, her left hand still in his right hand, glancing
again at the soft cloth glove, then looking directly into
his eyes: Yes, oh yes.

They rose, embraced for a long moment and stepped
back holding hands and looking into each other's eyes
as Yankee looked on. John Paul released her hands,

turned and walked away swiftly. Jan, her hands still held as if in his, watched him go. Then she sat down and buried her face in her arms on the table.

IX

Special from the *Euro Press Syndicate*

LONDON—A senior member of the EPS team has been placed on extended leave and barred from access to EPS facilities and operations under suspicion of masterminding a network of investigative reporters alleged to have delivered information obtained on background and from confidential sources to people suspected of high-level involvement in illegal drug and weapons sales. The charges are ripping through press rooms and government offices on three continents. EPS promises a full and thorough investigation and, if improprieties or illegalities have occurred, to fire or prosecute all who are involved.

"THANK YOU, AMOS," began Simon Stoddard as he moved to the conclusion of his post-op debriefing. "Despite the loss of Martín Santos, it proved to be most successful. The loss of Santos will be a temporary setback because the new administration in Mexico City appears to be cooperative. Exposing Thurston was very beneficial, and our hand in that has strengthened our position and that of Malcolm Garfield as he returns to his station with DEA. And, I appreciate your counsel as I wrestled with the opportunity to take a more active role in operation of the training facility and pharmaceutical plant. Having resumed my role as legal advisor and representative, I am breathing a bit more easily.

"There is, however, one last and most disconcerting item before we conclude. I have, upon most reliable authority, a cautionary tale not of our making but extremely pertinent to our activities. In his relationship with Ariana Lentz, Marcello Barcqe is exposed to danger and is endangering us. It seems that Ms. Lentz's association with Joselyn Prescott has created a pipeline into the offices of a most nefarious network of high-level executives in charge of financial and operational activities tied inextricably to international criminal behavior, especially drugs and weapons sales and transport. Prescott is an important link in an intelligence ring employing journalists to ferret out vital and timely information related to legitimate business enterprise and governmental regulatory and law enforcement policies and field operations. Wittingly or unwittingly, Ariana Lentz has been feeding the beast, transmitting to Prescott the findings she and Barcqe are compiling, both on and off the record. Ariana's restoration to journalistic prominence through her association with Marcello, and her access to his contacts, notes and drafts, are producing information and identifying sources that are finding their way into this intelligence network, perhaps to lead to exposure of the sources to 'offers they cannot refuse' in the well-known jargon of the past."

"And, Simon, you know this how?"

"Dear friend, there are matters that I dare not discuss even with you."

"More movement in the dancing landscape . . . Dear friend?"

"As you well know, Amos, in this game of musical chairs, the music never stops . . . except, of course, when it does. It is most important that one is not the last man standing when the music stops."

"Simon, have you something for me in this matter?"

"Yes. If you will arrange your rare book expeditions most judiciously, you might watch over our friend, Marcello, and his consort, Ariana, and especially her growing relationship with Joselyn Prescott. If you can peer into Prescott's associations with the upper one-tenth of one percent, by all means do so. But, and I mean this Amos, do not, I say again *not*, get too close to the flames. Do not get burned this time, Amos. It would most assuredly prove fatal."

"And my associates?"

"Leave Devon out of this for now. If our examination proves true, we will want him to deal the hand to Malcolm. When the time comes, if it comes, I will talk with Marcello."

Turning to gaze into his *Deus Ex Machina*, Simon continued, "Amos, I am beginning to think about focusing more on my firm's business with the international community. We may wish to approach these gray matters at a more leisurely pace in the future, leave the crusading to Devon and Malcolm who are younger and still imbued with thoughts of winning the wars on drugs and terrorism. Who knows, winning might be a pleasure worth pursuing but I doubt it, the winning that is. When, and I think it is a matter of *when* rather than *if*, terrorism mingles with cartel cash, we might be well advised to sit it out.

Ariana Lentz sat comfortably with Joselyn Prescott in Joselyn's posh London office, explaining the network of contacts she and Marcello Barcqe had forged in Latin America and linked with well-placed members of public, private and non-profit organizations in North America and Europe. The network was virtually invisible because it focused upon influential assistants and associates rather than the much more visible principals they served. Working just beneath the placid surface of these organizations, Ariana and Marcello acquired intimate details of their inner workings, generally on background and guaranteeing anonymity, and access to their principals for on-record interviews. A few loops in the network she described illuminated dark areas where "unnamed officials" authorized and oversaw "plausibly deniable" activities legitimated by "authorities having jurisdiction." Prescott had shown particular interest in activities that meandered along the boundaries of journalistic propriety, ethics and legality, but, though wary, Ariana was anxious to appear to have regained her previous place among the best of those reporting from within the labyrinth of international crime and terrorism.

"Ariana, you and I have an excellent track record together. We have scooped the competition several times in the last year or so, and your features have been received very well by our more sophisticated readers. Marcello's contributions have deepened their confidence in your work, but it has been your range of experience spanning two generations of terrorist activity that has sealed the deal with those who have risen to power during the last couple of decades. They are in charge now and they want to know things that lie beyond the horizons of our general readers. Recently, a select group of us has offered them a special subscription service: a line of reporting and analysis that reaches far deeper than today's news and back-page features. As the managing editor of our group and with the approval of our subscribers, I have been authorized to offer you membership in our reportorial group. The standards for membership are very stringent, and loss of confidence in performance may result in severe consequences. I recommend that you think very carefully before you respond to this offer.

"Does the offer include Marcello?"

"Not at this time. The readership is currently focused upon the EU, but its interests extend to intercontinental activities that significantly impinge upon Europe and the UK, so the future is not cast in concrete."

"How long is the offer on the table?"

"Twenty-four hours. If you indicate interest, I will specify a not-later-than response time at the close of our conversation."

"May I consult with others during my deliberations?"

"No. This conversation is strictly between us. Some of my colleagues get quite nervous at this stage of negotiations. The offer is not ever tendered to anyone who is not familiar with the full nature of such confidences."

"Thank you, Joselyn. I am both honored and flattered. I shall reply well within your time frame."

Twelve hour later, Joselyn Prescott received a brief encrypted text message containing Ariana Lentz's acceptance of the offer and confirmation of her full understanding of the conditions of the appointment.

"I accept what you say," murmured Simon Stoddard as he gazed into the far reaches of his exquisite *Deus Ex Machina*. Amos Sanson had just finished a status report on his watch over Joselyn Prescott and Ariana Lentz.

Turning to face Amos, Simon replied, "I will take no action for now. When may I expect a report meeting your exacting standards?"

"We are close, Simon. I will ask Rosada to send you updates, but I prefer details to await our conversation here. Her communications must be short and cryptic, and I want no loose ends that we may have to cope with later."

Early, on a beautiful day just hours after leaving Simon Stoddard's office, Sanson breakfasted with Jack Kavanaugh and Lillian Vizcaya in a café overlooking the Bay of Biscay. Amos opened their conversation with an overview of the concerns he shared with Simon. During the briefing, Jack and Lillian had exchanged glances, so Amos was looking forward to what they would say.

"Close associates in London have suggested that certain high-level industrial and political interests are rumored to be particularly well informed these days," began Irish Jack. Picking up the conversation, Lillian added, "Discussions with some of our industrialists have expressed concern that a small group of London insiders is stealing a march on the EU. Perhaps Jack and I should visit the UK for a bit of look and listen."

Sanson interjected, "Simon is somewhat worried that you two should not be noticed there just now."

"Simon is always 'somewhat worried' about something or other," replied Jack with his typical Irish grin and lilt in his voice. "The lads have been pretty cooperative for a while, and folks from Madrid's upper echelons are vacationing along the bay with growing frequency. ETA and the PIRA appear to be out-of-sight, out-of-mind, for the moment, perhaps because drug cartels and Islamic terrorists have shunted them off the stage."

"Jack and I have not taken the boat out for a while. A trip across the Channel would be invigorating this time of year."

"I understand; however, their general heightened level of security may challenge your usual degree of situational awareness," replied Amos.

"Ah," exclaimed Jack with a quiet intensity. "A tradecraft field exercise. Are we up to it, dear Lillian?"

"How shall we know if we don't set sail?" inquired Lillian with mock sincerity.

"Amos, we promise a heightened level of situational awareness to more than match their heightened level of security, and a thorough report at this table at this time next week."

"Until next week then, vaya con Díos." Sanson rose and departed, saying softly to himself, "They will not resist a challenge. There are some characteristics of those devoted to *the cause* that invariably stretch the bounds of caution."

For a week, Sanson melded into the varied landscapes of Iberia. He had not traveled simply for pleasure for some time, so for a few days that passed all too quickly, he roamed along the pathways of the mythical knight-errant, Don Quixote de La Mancha. Some spots do not change.

"Your concerns are well founded," began Lillian Vizcaya while Irish Jack and Amos sipped café con leche and listened intently in the predawn gloom of the café overlooking the bay. "The arrangements are arcane, the security measures are broad and deep. The network is extensive, the product is very highly regarded, the patrons can easily afford the expenses. The legal base for the organization, an international non-profit research and education foundation, is described as 'impeccable, owing in large measure to the quality of the work and reputation of the DC-area attorney of record.' While the organization is highly secretive it is legitimate, and its principal patrons include leading industrialists and financiers across the globe. They can afford the best, they are capable of recognizing the best when they see it, they will settle for nothing less. Joselyn Prescott is well thought of, but she is not at the pinnacle of the operational framework. There does appear to be a significant subset of the customer base that plays in the gray areas and on the dark side. And, Ariana Lentz has replied affirmatively to Prescott's offer."

Sanson asked, "How confident are you in the sources and the information?"

After a brief pause, Vizcaya replied, "I cannot judge the quality of the information because I am not fully aware of the situation; however, the sources are highly reliable. With that in mind, I believe the report to be likely. Those of you who understand the situation will have to judge the true value of the information for yourselves."

Leaning forward, Jack whispered, "Lillian, explain to Amos, without burdening him with too much detail, why we have such high regard for the sources."

Lillian motioned to the gentle soul lingering out of earshot behind the bar for another cup of coffee, sweet with warm milk. After the waiter placed the steaming cup in front of her and returned to his place from which he could see the cobbled avenue between the café and the low parapet overlooking the bay, she responded to Jack's suggestion, "Some who have first-generation links to others having long-time associations are permitted access to a few who have survived a lifetime in the shadows. Among them are some who play significant roles on and beneath the surface of current affairs including but not limited to those we have been discussing. We trust them, they trust us, our lives depend upon this trust."

Looking more at Jack than at Amos, Lillian inquired, "Then, Amos, you will discuss with our mutual patron the importance of the pathways down which Ms. Lentz treads?"

"And," added Jack, "do so with utmost discretion."

"Yes," replied Amos. "The dangers to all of us are apparent. Our agenda is concluded?"

Smiling as he replied, Jack said, "We have a bit of a bonus for you, Amos. While Lillian flitted from here to there, I visited a mutual friend. The special pharmaceutical facilities near Bilboa have come online. As such facilities tend to do, they added several internships to the R&D activities. We don't know who is filling these

positions, but Lil and I thought you might be interested in these photographs." As Amos leafed through
the couple of dozen photos, Jack continued, "They con-
stitute a mixed group. Some are young graduates of
French and German practical science and engineering
programs, and a sprinkling are somewhat older men
and women whose nationalities we do not know. Some
appear to be of Mediterranean descent, some Latino,
two or three are European or North American. We are
confident that you will find some use for the photographs."

"We hope you will not think it presumptuous of us
to add to this morning's agenda," added Lillian with a
slight smile.

"No. Such surprises brighten one's day."

"By the way, Amos," asked Jack, "how was your foray
into our beautiful countryside?"

"Profitable, I believe, but I'll know more when I visit
Guanajuato next week."

Rising, Sanson extended a hand to each of them.
Jack firmly grasped his left hand; Lillian, softly his
gloved right hand. As Amos walked into the dawn sun,
his back to them, he appeared to raise his right hand.
Lillian murmured, "Softening a bit?" Irish Jack whispered, "Ever the romantic, dear Lillian."

"In summary, Simon, it may be worse than you suspected. My inquiries were sufficient to cause angst over
conversations with Marcello. He has been useful, but I
and several of my associates do not want to work with
him while he is collaborating with Lentz. Prescott's
role with this foundation is clear, and Ariana Lentz

is in her stable. I cannot tell you how far the system extends; mine is but one of your many theaters of operations. And, though the legal construct may appear unassailable, I can only speculate about its vulnerabilities to special investigations. Risks abound, and savvy risk management suggests that we sever connections with Lentz, including, under current arrangements, Marcello Barcqe."

"Thank you, Amos. The report, disturbing as it is, is what I asked for."

As Sanson departed, Stoddard punched a single key on his phone and, after a moment, began to speak jovially, "Marcello, Simon Stoddard here. Some very important information has come to me and I wish to share it with you at the earliest possible moment . . . No, it cannot be discussed over the phone. Will you be in my vicinity anytime soon? . . . Excellent! Fredericksburg at the usual time . . . Chau, Marcello, cuídate."

Malcolm Garfield concluded his briefing for Devon Xander on the current state of affairs in Mexico, "Turmoil along our southwestern border, increasing violence along the Gulf, upticks in the quality of their tactical leadership and operations, more and better information and decision-making. The cartels are maturing, just as the Mafia did during Prohibition, and I think the drug guys are smarter and have modern technology. We take down one of their leaders, a new guy steps up, and two out of three are better than the guys they're replacing. Some of them are SWAT veterans or PMF vets with multiple tours. They're sort of like germs getting more resistant to antibiotics, the new ones are tougher than the ones who go down. More sophisticated at the top, more savvy and savage on the streets. If we get real lucky, maybe they'll kill themselves off.

"But we're getting better too. They move, we hit, they retaliate, and the beat goes on. Our drones help with surveillance, but I wish we could send 'em in 'runnin' hot.' But even with asset forfeiture, they have more cash in the till."

When Garfield paused for a moment, Xander spoke up. "Some reports out of the EU say a secret think tank serving up high-quality information to select government and industrial leaders is finding its way to the cartels, maybe even to terrorists."

Malcolm cut in, "Evidence, damn it, we need hard evidence! Justice wants to prosecute. Homeland Security will settle for 'actionable,' but our guys want a slam dunk before they'll stretch. Will you be seeing Amos at any time soon, or is he still off chasing the ghost of Don Quixote?"

"Nothing scheduled, but I'm seeing Simon before I leave town. And, I'll talk with Rosada when I get home. She has ways to get in touch with Amos. I'll call if I get anything solid . . . make that anything, because nothing about that think tank seems solid."

Next day, Devon advised Malcolm not to share anything sensitive with Marcello Barcqe, and absolutely nothing with Ariana Lentz.

"It is good to see you again, my friend," said the old bookseller in Guanajuato as he recognized the man standing in the doorway to his shop. "I have looked for you each noon since receiving your letter from Spain.

Come, let us walk to the café for refreshments, where you can tell me about your ramblings along the path of the real Don Quixote."

After relating highlights of his journey, Amos Sanson guided the conversation toward other topics. Diverting a bit reluctantly, Señor Alvaria-Iverson replied to Sanson's questions with sufficient detail that only occasionally were follow-up questions required and offered his opinions only when asked. His devotion to Rosada Ángel Jesús prompted him to cooperate as best he could.

As the afternoon shadows lengthened, Don Quixote brought the conversation to a turn. "Since the end of the 19th century, US interests have brought regime change in many places, and the interests of those places seemed to matter little in the exchange. What I hear in our streets and plazas, simplified so as to be understood by the common people, is 'we'll let you do it our way; otherwise, you're on your own as long as you don't get in our way.' The simplification generally is not in your best interests.

"As we are both men of books in the modern information age, allow me to offer this: What we must do today may be dictated by something done yesterday, and we may have to do tomorrow something already set in motion, perhaps unintentionally. People, good and bad, will fight with the resources at hand, and surprise is a principle practiced by all.

"In our remaining time together, let us turn back to your journey along the hero's path, the path of el hidalgo ingenioso, Don Quixote de La Mancha."

And so they did, sometimes leaning forward

intently, often leaning back to laugh quietly . . . two old friends enjoying a light red wine of local vintage and the companionship of books.

Ariana Lentz and Marcello Barcqe finished briefing each other on their recent trips abroad. They were satisfied with their findings and were confident that they had enough to polish their work and go to press.

After a pause, Marcello laid one more item on the table: "Ariana, our very fruitful and financially rewarding association must come to an end."

Incredulously, Ariana responded, "Come to an end! What do you mean? Have I missed something?"

"A couple of things have come up recently. First, I am leaving journalism for a while. The new government in Mexico City has asked me to join our embassy staff in Washington. I have accepted the offer."

"You accepted without so much as a heads-up in a matter in which I have a major stake?"

"The opportunity came my way out of the blue, and they pressed me for an immediate decision."

"I'd like, in fact I insist upon, an explanation!"

"Their reasoning goes something like this: they need an 'astute'—their word—observer who knows the Americans, who knows the issues and has enough special operations experience to understand both covert action and militarization of law enforcement in addition to our trade and anti-drug relationships. Caught in a trap of my own making, Ariana. It is the success of my, and our, investigative reporting that brought them to my door. I fit the suit they've tailored, and I want to try it on."

"I can understand that, Marcello. What I'm having trouble with is you not giving me so much as a hint that this was coming."

"That, Ariana, brings me to the second topic in this couplet."

"Pray tell, while you are in a sharing mood," said Ariana with more than just a touch of sarcasm.

Pausing, a bit for emphasis, a bit to gather his thoughts, Marcello spoke with bitterness discernible in his voice. "I have been apprised of your deepening association with Joselyn Prescott, an association that tramples the ethics of journalism and likely some laws, and which you chose not to share with me, though I have a major stake in it. As you well know, the role of a free press is protected by the Constitution in America. They define it as a right that the press is obliged to honor, and for which the press receives legal protections. Joselyn Prescott directs a strategic information service that not only provides expert analysis and operational advice but shares information obtained through mutually agreed confidences and on background. In my professional opinion, and in a growing number of legal opinions, the information she provides to a select few 'clients' is obtained fraudulently and in violation of the sanctity of the press. She is an intelligence agent motivated by money and ego, serving interests inimical to society.

"Damn it, Ariana, I don't mean to be pedantic. Stuff we've put together has appeared in some highly questionable insider reports that have landed on the desks of some highly questionable people in some highly questionable enterprises, with our names on them and our reputations substantiating them, and without so much as a heads-up or a hint that you were selling us . . . me . . . out to Prescott's puppet masters.

"I don't insist upon an explanation. The betrayal has gone far beyond mere explanation. You've killed the goose that lays golden eggs. People I've known for years have slammed their doors in my face. For a while at least, forever perhaps, my journalistic goose is cooked. Hopefully, our book deal is not off. Hell, the way things go these days, the book deal may be better than ever. But as a team of investigative journalists, our goose is cooked, deep-fat fried, boiled and broiled!"

Continuing in a more subdued manner, Marcello capped the revelation: "I am happy to have been offered the post in Washington. I need time to get back on track. For a while, I'll just be a back-office analyst in the trade, a consultant to those who still trust me but furnishing information and conclusions within a controlled system of facts, verified and edited, working for others but hopefully still thinking for myself.

"That's it, case closed, bon voyage."

"That's it? Case closed? Bon voyage? Who? Who told you this? How can you be so sure you can trust . . ."

"Trust?" Marcello exclaimed. "My sources top 'highly reliable.' My advice to you, Ariana, if you're still open to anything I might say, is to take your money and disappear for a while. All manner of shit is going to descend upon Prescott. Don't be around to share it. She has already been burned by those she thought would protect her, and the crap could stick to anyone close by."

In a lowered voice, Marcello, concluded sadly, "Get out of that game, Ariana, while you can." He was already walking away.

"By the way, Marcello, a rogue operation at EPS-London appears to have closed down," whispered Simon Stoddard as he stepped close, laid his left hand on Barcqe's right shoulder and shook his right hand after adding his own to the many kind "welcomes" at the close of a reception honoring new diplomatic officers to the Mexican Embassy in Washington. "It seems that the agent in charge was found in her apartment, deceased by way of a 9 mm bullet through her left temple, though as I understand it she was widely known as an accomplished right-handed amateur tennis player. She generally kept such a pistol in the center drawer of the teak desk in her study where she often worked long into the night. Someone cleaning the stables, I imagine, and sending a not-to-subtle message down the line? Her job as managing editor of EPS-London has been given to your old partner, Ariana Lentz, reward for the excellent work the two of you shared, I suppose.

"Again, old friend, welcome back. I shall look forward to seeing more of you during your time in Washington."

X

An Irreplaceable Literary Life Lost

*(EPS, LONDON) A man of letters known inti-
mately to very few outside his native country, but
whose tragic death is mourned deeply throughout
the Spanish-speaking literary world, was honored
recently in Guanajuato, Mexico. Rosada Ángel Jesús,
his "La Aprendiza," delivered an emotional eulogy
to a tearful congregation that flowed out of the old
neighborhood church onto the narrow street near his
bookshop. Don Quixote Alvaria-Iverson, whose early
writings have been revived during current debates
regarding the wars on drugs and terrorism and popular Mexican opposition to US unilateral actions on
Mexican soil, is believed to have been targeted by
several of the warring factions. Mexican authorities
promise a thorough investigation of Alvaria-Iverson's "assassination." Officials in the US embassy in
Mexico City have not responded to questions directed
to them by international journalists.*

"SO, YOU HAVE DEVELOPED AN INTEREST in the 19th-century writings regarding the early explorations of hidden Meso-
american cities?"

"A commercial interest, mi amigo." Amos Sanson
and Don Quixote Alvaria-Iverson were sipping coffee

following lunch at the cantina near DQ's shop in Guanajuato. Sanson was looking for drafts of books published during the early investigations of Mayan cities first revealed by Bishop Diego de Landa, later popularized by Prescott, Caddy and Walker, and Stephens and Catherwood, and had casually mixed in a question about a mutual acquaintance, Carlos Casadea.

"Commercial, of course," replied DQ. He was well aware that Amos Sanson's inquiries often combined personal interests with commercial enterprise, a practice quite common among those who searched for rare manuscripts. "About your inquiry concerning the gentleman engaged quietly in discussions crucial to continuation of the North American Free Trade Association, and who shares with us a fondness for words, I shall simply quote Henrik Ibsen: 'Look into any man's heart you please, and you will always find, in every one, at least one black spot which he has to keep concealed.'" A thoughtful pause, then, "And some spots don't change."

Don Quixote's voice faded, his eyes slowly closed, a red dot in the center of his traditional white cotton blouse blossomed into a crimson circle as his chin came to rest upon his chest, the brilliant crimson barely distinguishable from the embroidery on his brightly colored vest. He appeared to have nodded off, a familiar siesta at the end of a simple lunch and a glass of light red wine.

His companion, however, casually but quickly rose from his chair and moved directly to the wall of the building across the narrow street leading from the bookshop to the café. Close against the wall, Sanson moved away from the café, turning at the first corner and again at the next corner, there to wait and watch.

Soon, two men emerged from a door to the building across from the café, one of them carrying a hard-shell briefcase such as might contain a disassembled rifle. They glanced both ways, turned toward Sanson and walked past without noticing him, both with heads and eyes lowered. But he saw them clearly. He would not forget the assassins of Don Quixote Alvaria-Iverson.

In about half an hour, a waiter approached to awaken the old man and send him back to his shop. What followed spread quickly throughout the neighborhood, and later deliberately from continent to continent. The reaction was both outrage and sadness. Police from Guanajuato to Mexico City and journalists from Latin America to Spain pursued various paths, following the influence of Alvaria-Iverson's writings from his activism of the past into the chaos of the present.

Rosada Ángel Jesús was inconsolable.

A week later, at a late dinner with Simon Stoddard after a long day with Malcolm Garfield, Devon Xander was interrupted in midsentence by a unique ring on his secure satellite phone marking an urgent call from Malcolm. Devon answered, listened quietly for several minutes, closed the phone and put it in his pocket. He turned to Simon and summarized the call: "One of Malcolm's Interpol associates in Marseille told him that two "accountants" for a Spanish security firm working for a pharmaceutical plant in Bilboa were found staked out with wire in a hog finishing lot last night. They were identified by a few fingerprints and a scattering of DNA. The wires had cut into the bone, and Interpol thinks they were left alive as a late snack for the hogs. They were suspected wet ops guys, and Interpol thinks they are connected with the hit on Alvaria-Iverson in Guanajuato."

Simon swiveled his chair until he was facing his *Deus Ex Machina*. After a moment, he said softly, "Just because he prefers silence and fog, don't ever forget that he is equally adept at sound and fury." He turned back toward Devon, and their conversation continued as if it had not been interrupted.

XI

END OF THE RAINBOW

The Appalachian Springs *Weekly Informer*

APPALACHIAN SPRINGS—Janet Sterling Trent passed away quietly in her sleep after a long illness that forced her retirement from a Capital City law firm and return to Appalachian Springs five years ago to create and direct the Appalachian Springs Community Foundation. Trent was preceded in death by her father, former State Senator Augustus Trent, and her mother, Martha Sterling Trent. Ms. Trent's remains will be cremated and her ashes scattered over the graves of her parents. Funeral arrangements and plans for a memorial service are incomplete at this time.

ENTERING YANKEE'S TWO MONTHS LATER, John Paul Anderson met only apparitions at the round table (four appearing not to have aged during the decades since he last saw them, Jan looking as she had two months ago, sitting in their regular places).

Yankee: Well I'll be damned, John Paul, haven't seen you for a year of Sundays and then I see you twice in the last couple of months.

John Paul: Hey, Yankee. Who's leading the American League East these days, the Red Sox?

Yankee: The Red Sox! Bite your tongue, mystery man. What'll you have?

John Paul: A light red wine of local vintage, my friend. Have you seen Jan? I'm supposed to meet her here today.

Yankee: Jan . . . She passed away about three weeks ago. Heart failure. Stress, that's what gets 'em while they still have a lot of livin' to do. She was a great lawyer, defended the poor and downtrodden while bossin' the biggest corporate law firm in the state. She came home to lead our community foundation . . . accomplished a lot of good things. She was quite a lady.

John Paul picked up the glass of wine Yankee placed on the bar near his gloved right hand, turned, walked slowly to the table, stood behind his old seat, looked at each empty chair, paused at Jan's chair and said as if to himself: You didn't say. You asked me not to go, but you didn't say.

John Paul lifted his glass: Gone. You're all gone. The irony of it! You who played so graciously upon this stage, leaving your legacies of light while I skulked through the shadows from role to role, from deceit to deceit, from lie to lie, weaving destructions into my web.

John Paul paused, then continued: You were my safe anchorage, my North Star, the home that kept me sane. Where is the hand of Almighty God in your dying and my surviving? Alone. Alone? With memories of your modest mendacities and magnificent merits meandering through my mind . . . with the bittersweet of your lives enshrined in the past while mine looms somewhere in the fog. I *shall* see you again, in another dimension where we *will* sit together and relate our lives lived out in the passing of time, telling not less than all the truths, nor more . . . and renewing abiding love. Thomas Wolfe said we can't go home again. But we *are* home again, as you have been throughout the years, memories in our minds mingling with feelings in our hearts. We are forever home again.

John Paul raised the glass to his lips, drank, placed the glass on the table, turned slowly, nodded to Yankee, and trudged into the darkness as if weighed down by a heavy burden.

Yankee, eyes on John Paul as he walked away, slowly dried a glass, then turned away from the bar and placed the glass beside others on the shelf.

XII

Special to the *Sunday Sentinel* Book Reviews
by *Marcello Barcqe*

*(GUANAJUATO, MEXICO) Antonio Cardoza, expert
in the preservation and restoration of ancient manuscripts and art, and the long-time partner of Don
Quixote Alvaria-Iverson, announced his partnership with Amos Sanson, a little-known but highly
respected rare-book finder and a close friend and
business associate of Alvaria-Iverson. Sanson will
join Cardoza in Guanajuato and will focus on consignment searches while retaining his interests in
bookstores in the US Midwest.*

ON A RAINY DAY a week later, Simon Stoddard sat at a corner table in a historic pub in Fredericksburg, Virginia,
watching as a nondescript gentleman moved quietly
through the thinning lunch crowd to pause in front of
him and nod. Simon gestured toward the empty seat
beside him. The gentleman sat and when the waiter
approached to take his order said simply, "A light red
wine of local vintage, if you please." After the waiter
placed the glass of wine on the table and departed,
the gentleman lifted it in silent salute with a hand

encased in a soft, cloth glove that matched in color the raincoat he was wearing.

"You are a hard man to find when you do not wish to be found," began Simon. "May I assume then that I found you so easily because you decided so?"

"Perspicacious as always, Simon."

"You're sure?"

A moment passed while the gentleman sipped his wine and appeared to search his mind.

"I am sure," he replied softly.

"Then while we await lunch, I shall begin a tale that I think you will find intriguing and familiar. Carlos Casadea . . ."

The End?

POEMS

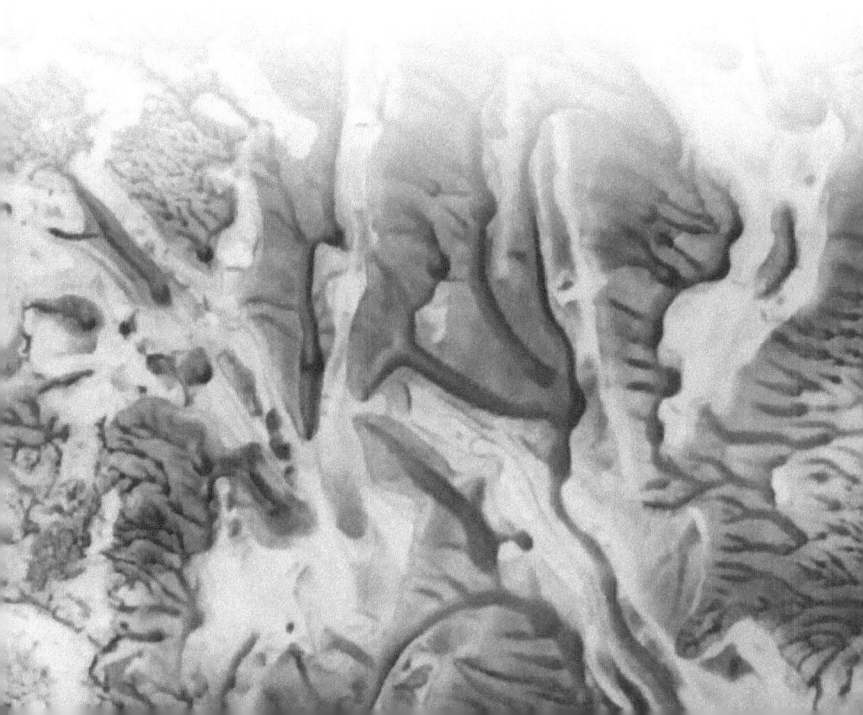

AUTHOR'S NOTE

"The Master Mysterian"*

This poem preceded all the other works in this volume; it was part of the immediate post-retirement period that ended my working for a living and initiated my working on living.

Having been a member of the Baker Street Irregulars for a while, I set out to reread the Sherlock Holmes stories, compose a poem encapsulating Holmes's career as the world's first consulting detective, and add my own take on what he did after falling locked in battle with his arch nemesis, Professor Moriarty, into "the treacherous, swollen torrent" at the falls of Reichenbach.

The excellent illustrations by Sidney Paget in "The Adventure of the Final Problem" suggest a remarkable physical likeness between Holmes and Moriarty—Moriarty appearing to be a bit older—and that they were as well matched in physical combat as during their intellectual duels.

---

* Constructed of two terms, *viz*. (1) mystery, n., a work of fiction concerned with the identification and capture of a criminal or criminals; and (2)-ian, var. of -an, a suffix meaning, of or belonging to, e.g., Humanitarian.

"Finding Genre"

As one thing often leads to another, I was introduced to C. Auguste Dupin, featured in three stories written by Edgar Allan Poe between 1841 and 1844, and thought to be the original model for the detective in literature. Poe had created Dupin sometime before the word "detective" had been coined to define the profession that was to become a staple in law enforcement, investigation (factual and fictional), and among the reading public.

"Reality"

During the last century, words serving us through mass and specialized media have illuminated our progression from dependence upon facts to reliance upon opinions for much of our daily evidence-seeking and decision-making . . . perhaps it has ever been so. We are deluged with information in such quantity, variety, and rapidity that we hardly have time to consider whether the information is worth the words spoken or written with it. Polls, the results of which have become staples in the chain of information meant to inform, convince or turn us this way or that, have almost become the only dots we can connect on our way to enlightenment . . . our search for reality.

"Spoils of War"

From the American Civil War have come two letters that, while perhaps closer to prose than poetry, display wonderful and poetic simplicity, artfulness, and beauty while leaving no doubts regarding the human costs of war: Sullivan Ballou's letter to Sarah, and Abraham Lincoln's letter to Mrs. Bixby. In nearly all who have given thought to the art and craft of war, there lurks a poem of war. This is mine.

"Visitation"

Death is a fact of life and has a special place in poetry. A trip through an old cemetery provides many examples of the meaning of death, and of life, carved into stone at the heads of graves and into the hearts of men. Though the pain may fade with time, the fact remains forever—life so significant brought to an end with death so natural to all living things.

THE MASTER MYSTERIAN
A NARRATIVE IN VERSE CELEBRATING
THE WAY OF MR. SHERLOCK HOLMES

Prelude

Happening on a crisp, clear day
Near equinox the season
Chancing upon mounds of clay
With which to fashion reason

From clay to bricks and bricks to house
A house quite amply roomed
And in each room a memoir vouched
Of evidence entombed

The Story

Serpents, hounds, and criminal minds
Find success when first applied
Bend unto the master's will
When he detects the facts that hide

Observe and listen, we surmise
And work with tools well honed
For it's unwise to theorize
Before the facts are known

Skilled in arts arcane and manly
Strength enough to bend cold steel
Able when engaged in combat
Sensing music's soothing feel

Frugal in both thought and substance
Wasting little time and treasure
Listening, then expounding wisdom
Pocketing fees in equal measure

Aloof and cool and so exacting
Curious to relentless fault
Bending not to foundless guessing
Trusting in the power of thought

Composed in manner, and deceptive
Seeking facts to theorize
Reasoning and observing coldly
Admiring she who pierced his guise

Escaping commonplace at times
Though it provides most puzzling myst'ry
Forcing him to seek himself
While spying in the enemy's country

Signature of a typ-e-writer
Behind which foulest criminal hides
A thing so small may tip the scale
And clearly show the hand that guides

With him on whom he could rely
Tracing paths o'er land, 'mongst trees
Objecting to secure just outcome
In courts superior to the Assize

Into the mists of fog and time
Fell the foemen locked in war
Lost to all who so admired them
Drawn untracked to places far

From the mists emerged but one
Lost to all though still sublime
Exiting from a shop on Church Street
To reassert his place in time

The antidote I seek, said he
Is arcane work of cryptic test
Shrouded such that claims one's mind
And brings the breaking brain to rest

His tools at hand, his mind secure
Trying and absorbed at times
Witchcraft complementing genius
Patiently to frustrate crimes

A Toast

Gentlemen, ladies, colleagues, guests
Attend we to his rich bequests
Say we all, in honor rests
He who stood against all tests:
Mr. Sherlock Holmes

FINDING GENRE

Dupin, then Holmes, came first in time
Attracted to most baffling crime
They intent on finding facts
Illuminating criminal acts

Both were keen of mind and thinking
Nor from deeds to be found shrinking
Always they were logic bound
Reasoning from the facts they found

Both in patient observation
Nor deterred from innovation
Often tramping arcane mazes
Following paths each quarry blazes

Together they would forge a role
And claim a literary pole
Later sought by writers loyal
To paths pioneered by Poe and Doyle

REALITY

Faces in a crowd
No longer real
None of them average
All at some variance
From some measure of central tendency
Within some decile or quintile or quarter or half
Or 90 percent or 10 percent
Or one percent or one-tenth of one percent
Or just outside the one percent
In the newly found 95th to 99th percent
Whose wealth or household income
Is rising faster
Or falling faster
Or simply flat
Depending on how they were measured
Or how they were aggregated
Or what algorithm they were threaded through
Or how they were trending
Or the conclusions drawn from them
Or where they stood while an analyst explained them
No longer what they were
But not yet become
Until someone said they symbolized . . . something
Ignoring that once upon a time
They had been faces in a crowd

SPOILS OF WAR

When I think of it
I think of glory
And of duty, honor, country

And I think of nineteen-year-olds
Who will never, ever, for all eternity
Be twenty-year-olds
And I think of thirty-year-olds
Who talk quietly and cry quietly
And I want to cry too

But I can't; I didn't earn it.
They did.

They earned it with pieces of themselves
And pieces of their friends
And pieces of strangers
Who will never, ever, for all eternity
Be their friends

God bless them
And keep them
And be their friend
Forsaking them never, ever, for all eternity
For they deserve it

VISITATION

Death had come quietly with the night.

I am sorry for your loss; how are you doing?

I pause, then reply as quietly as death had come:
Death and I are reconciled.
We have watched together as time has passed
as naturally as birth commenced the lives
that brought us together.
Even stars born long ago
and being born as we have been
are visited in time by death
who will one day come for me.
As death is with life,
Death and I are reconciled.

PLAYS

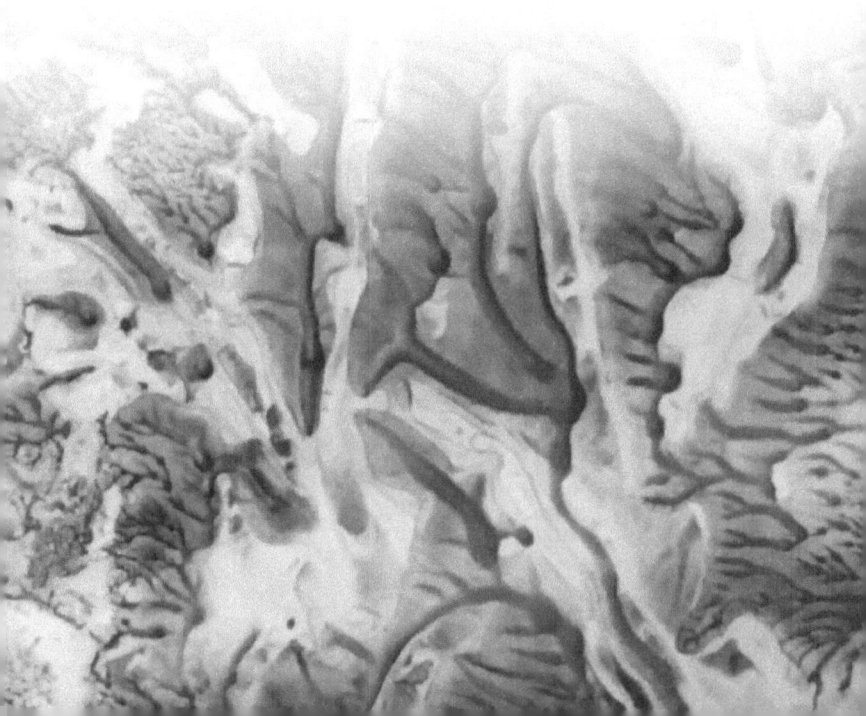

AUTHOR'S NOTE

*"I have always had a fancy that learning might
be made a play and recreation to children, and
that they may be brought to desire to be taught,
if it were proposed to them as a thing of honor,
credit, delight, and recreation, or as a reward
for doing something else; and if they were never
chided or corrected for the neglect of it."*
— John Locke, Esq.

WE BEGIN WITH *The Time Machine,* a one-act, three-scene
play designed to augment middle- or high-school stud-
ies of the industrial revolution and regional economic
development in American history, perhaps as part of a
multi-disciplinary STEM/STEAM curriculum aimed at
current issues in society, science, and technology. The
structure and number of characters provide flexibility
for involving different numbers of students. The narratives add to the number of students who may participate. The play is also suitable for staged readings, in or
out of costume, and easily managed for presentation
by older students to younger ones.

The second play, *Parlor Games,* examines the nature

of gossip, rumor, and communication. It is appropriate for a variety of audiences, and its performance easily accommodates to a repertoire for busy agendas and student drama tournaments.

Both plays are suitable for staged readings, in costume or common dress, and fully staged productions.

THE TIME MACHINE
THE MONONGAHELA RIVER IN A CHANGING NATION

*When you put your hand in a flowing stream,
you touch the last that has gone before
and the first that is still to come.*
—Leonardo da Vinci

Synopsis:
This is a one-act, three-scene dramatization of development along the Monongahela River during the growth
of the United States from the 18th to the 21st centuries.
The scenes are set in the mid-18th, 19th, and 20th centuries, and describe the significance of the Mississippi–
Ohio–Monongahela river system for life along the
Monongahela River during three challenging periods
in American history. The brief narratives connect the
scenes to provide a history of growing communities
and technologies, internal conflict, and widening differences between advocates of industrial development
and environmental protection.

The play follows two families, the McKenzies and
the Bransons, as they experience the growth of a community. Over the years, members of the two families

agree and differ over the form of development along the river.

Economic development presents a paradox. On the one hand, it provides opportunities to improve our lives; on the other hand, it produces threats to the quality of our lives. This play casts light onto the paradox by illuminating some of the benefits and costs in words rather than numbers. The outcomes have physical, qualitative, and quantitative dimensions; dealing with them, however, is a person-to-person enterprise.

Structure:
Narration 1. Introduction
Scene 1, A Nation Beginning
Narration 2. c. 1750–1850
Scene 2, A Nation Growing
Narration 3. c. 1850–1950
Scene 3, A Nation Preserved
Narration 4. Conclusion and Challenge:
Life on and along the Monongahela River, c. 1950–2050

NARRATION 1: INTRODUCTION

From Fairmont, West Virginia, the waters of the Monongahela River flow north to the Ohio River and thence south to the Gulf of Mexico, from the mountains of West Virginia to the seven seas, a pathway to the world.

During the early years of the 18th century, settlement west of the Appalachian Mountains was sparse. After the Revolutionary War (1776–1783), more European settlers entered western Pennsylvania and Virginia. The 19th century witnessed further population growth and the American Civil War. The Western world—Europe and the Americas—erupted in an Industrial Revolution heightening a continuous cycle of industrialization, urbanization, pollution, law, and regulation. In the 20th century, industrial development and motorization gained momentum, fueled in part by two world wars.

In early settlements, the nature and quantities of waste materials generated by few people and small-scale industrialization were limited. But, as populations grew and concentrated in larger towns and cities, and science and technology altered the types and increased the volumes of pollutants, disposing of human and industrial wastes became more problematic, and conflict between those promoting industrial development and those seeking to preserve the environment emerged and increased. Today, that conflict lies at the heart of nearly every decision to build or renovate our public and private infrastructure.

Rivers descend through time, constantly changing as rains fall and waters flow in a timeless cycle. So it is with life upon the banks of the watercourses, an ever-changing diorama of exploration, settlement, growth, decline . . .

SCENE 1: A NATION BEGINNING

Cast:

Joshua Branson, first settler at this site along the Monongahela River. He established the trading post and fort at Branson's Inlet, and provided a focal point for settlers to farm the rich valleys and rolling hills in the western territories and for provisioning trappers, explorers, and others forging west along the Monongahela–Ohio waterway.

Jonas Branson, Joshua's younger brother, who is trapping and exploring the upper West Fork of the Monongahela. Joshua had intended to stay with a friendly Indian clan throughout two years of trapping and exploring, and then to rejoin Joshua in developing the trading post and their extensive farm and forest holding.

Thom McKenzie, farmer on a large tract north of the fort along the Monongahela River, who also builds flatboats and keelboats for settlers and others moving west and looking for opportunities among the French and Spanish downriver toward New Orleans. With the return of his son from the French and Indian War, McKenzie intends to open a freight service to the east, using wagons that he takes in trade for the boats purchased by those moving west.

Martha McKenzie, Thom's wife, an educated and cultured woman, who presses for a school and church, and enlivens the small but growing community with her music and public readings of the literature of Europe and eastern America.

Belinda McKenzie, generally called Bell, Thom and Martha's teen-aged daughter. Bell is the image of her mother, beautiful and talented. She also is a child of the frontier, who rides and hunts as avidly as do the young men.

Benton McKenzie, Thom and Martha's twenty-two-year-old son, who has returned recently from service as a scout for British forces along the Monongahela and Allegheny Rivers during the French and Indian

War. Though they are boyhood friends, Jonas Branson and Benton McKenzie disagree over the nature of development of the region.

Simon Trent, a land surveyor, who is laying out parcels of land for sale in the vicinity of Branson's Inlet and along the Monongahela River and its tributaries.

Leaman Stanton, a lawyer and land agent, who partners with Simon Trent.

Setting:

A frontier trading post and provision store inside a refuge fort overlooking an inlet off the Monongahela River in the far western reach of the Pennsylvania and Virginia colonies of British America about the middle of the 18th century just after the end of the French and Indian War.

▪ ▪ ▪

JOSHUA, *standing near the door of his store and gazing out at the boat landing near the foot of a bluff on which stands Branson's Fort, speaking half to himself and half to his friends gathered near the warm fireplace in the early morning twilight.* Jonas should be along any day now. He said he would return this spring before the East Coast fur merchants arrive. They should be here soon.

THOM. How long was Jonas upriver this trip, Joshua?

JOSHUA. Two seasons. He planned to spend last summer exploring the upper reaches of the West Fork. He thinks the valleys are rich and ready for farming if the Indian fracas can be smoothed out.

LEAMAN. I have not been on the frontier long, but I hear constantly about problems with the Indians. Discussions back East deal more and more with the growing feeling that the colonies are not being treated fairly by the Crown. Some think that the common rights of Englishmen are being denied to us. Others argue that if we engage in conflict with the British, they will set their Indian allies upon us settlers west of the Appalachian Mountains.

BENTON. The British have strong allies among the Indians, and they do not hesitate to employ them if they believe it to be in their best interests.

THOM. It will be interesting to hear from Jonas when he returns from upriver. His time with the Indians, and your experiences during the war, should tell us much about Indian issues. Joshua and I have set our roots here where we have found opportunities for farming, commerce, and industry, and for trade with the Indians. Trent and Leaman are laying the base for creation of a real community. It appears— *Thom is interrupted when his daughter, Bell, bursts into the room.*

BELL. A canoe is coming into the inlet! I think it is Jonas.

All leap from their seats and move to the door, looking out toward the heavily laden canoe approaching the landing.

JOSHUA. It is Jonas, and his canoe is riding low. Looks like he had good luck upriver.

BELL. Hurry, Ben! Let's help Jonas beach the canoe.

Bell and Ben leave the room.

THOM, *chuckling.* Those boys will have a lot of catching up to do, Joshua. I think Bell won't mind having them around. She misses getting out to shoot bigger game. And they may be surprised to see that she has grown up a bit since they've been away.

Hand in hand with Ben and Jonas, Bell exuberantly draws them into the room. Much walking around, shaking hands, introducing Leaman Stanton and Simon Trent to Jonas. All are trying to talk with Jonas, while Bell stands next to Benton with her eyes riveted on Jonas. In a moment, the excitement settles, and Joshua welcomes his younger brother back.

JOSHUA. It is good to have you home, Jonas. We've much to talk about. And, we're all anxious to hear from you and Benton about activities up and down the Monongahela.

JONAS. I'm glad to be back. I've seen a lot to be optimistic about along the Tygart and West Fork, and I'm looking forward to hearing about Ben's experiences north to the Ohio and up the Allegheny.

THOM. And, we've been holding off a lot of decisions until you two returned.

LEAMAN. Simon has surveyed Joshua's and Thom's land grants, and we've been talking a lot about the press of settlers moving into this country and planning to continue to the Northwest Territory. We've even talked about building a town around Joshua's fort and Thom's boat manufactories. Maybe we can get together in the morning to discuss the future of this splendid country.

All but Joshua leave. Joshua follows them to the door, stands for a moment gazing out, then turns and walks toward the store counter. The lights grow dark, then brighten as Thom and Martha, Benton, Jonas, and Leaman return. It is the morning of the next day.

JOSHUA. Come in, warm yourselves, coffee is by the fire.

LEAMAN. Thank you, Joshua. The spring chill does penetrate these Eastern bones.

Ben and Jonas look at each other and chuckle.

BEN. Where Jonas and I have been the last few winters, this weather is downright balmy.

THOM. Let's get to it, boys. I've got to go up to Lewis's sawmill to check on a load of lumber.

LEAMAN. Right. Boys, the country hereabouts is about the best I've seen since coming west. Good soil and water, magnificent stands of timber, coal outcroppings that require very little excavation, and the river flowing down to the Three Rivers where I think a sizable city will build up. Thom, when you and Ben open that freight line to Cumberland, the Monongahela and the Potomac will be linked, and the connection will put Branson's Inlet in position to grow. I see no end to the potential for growth, and these vast lands will furnish the raw materials and absorb the castoff wastes for that growth. You are here first, so you will reap the great rewards of your adventurous spirits. Right now, though, we need to be thinking about securing those rewards and building a town. Simon, show these good folks what we've put together.

Simon steps to the counter and unrolls a plat of the area.

SIMON. Thanks, Leaman. Gentlemen and Mrs. McKenzie, for a beginning, I have scribed the boundaries of the Branson and McKenzie grants and laid out a number of parcels along the river, around Branson's Inlet, and up the creek from the inlet. The town, I suggest, should extend from Joshua's trading post and Thom's boat works a little way inland from the river. Thom's manufactories will draw industry into this area (*Points toward the plat.*), and commercial activity will develop around the trading post. Each area will include inns to accommodate visitors and newcomers. Houses with kitchen gardens for townspeople can spread out from the industrial and commercial areas along the river.

MARTHA. It is impressive, Mr. Trent. But where are the school and church, and where is a social hall where we can hold dances and other community events?

SIMON. Here, Mrs. McKenzie. (*Points toward the plat.*) This building can serve as school, church, social hall, and the circuit court when it comes this way. In time, it may become the center of community life for the town.

THOM. Splendid presentation, Simon. A town will attract travelers and provide trades and labor for our growing enterprise. However, I'm a bit concerned about this talk of independence and about the war parties that plague the outlying farms.

JONAS. I believe we can trade with the Indians and forge good relations with them.

BEN. That might be possible where you've been, Jonas, but I believe the Six Nations will parley with the British. If the talk of independence leads to war with the redcoats, their Indian allies will likely raid hard up and down the frontier.

JONAS. If that's the case, Ben, then we had best look to our farms. If they see that we respect and are willing to share the land, they . . . at least some of them . . . will side with us.

BEN. Farms are important, but they are only part of our growth and wealth. We will need our mills and manufactories to build up our communities.

To keep them working and to support the forces required to protect them, we need to harvest the coal and timber.

JOSHUA. In any case, the fort will provide refuge for people living in this area, and a town might be big enough to warrant a militia, maybe even a detachment of regular soldiers. The road back east and Thom's freight line will make it easier to support detachments along the frontier. We are the arms of a growing America reaching out to the West. Our fingertips are the trappers, explorers, and others who are searching out the pathways settlers will follow as America moves west. One day, we'll be the heart of a vast and prosperous country, and this river will be one of the great arteries that carries us forward.

LEAMAN. Gentlemen, and Mrs. McKenzie, upon this wilderness cornucopia will be built thriving communities and great fortunes. Industry, commerce, agriculture, wealth—all lie in the future for those who seize their opportunities and found their own destinies.

THOM. Though we sometimes differ on particulars, Joshua and I see eye to eye on the prospects for our community. This country is grand enough for farms and mills and shops. We'll be able to provide lumber, coal, and food enough to fuel our own growth and trade with the Eastern seaboard and down river to New Orleans, maybe beyond. Never will we be compelled to endure the degradation that afflicts cities in Europe and along the Eastern seaboard. The bounty of this land will last forever, and in it we and our posterity shall forever flourish.

End, Scene 1

NARRATION 2

c. 1750–1850

During the late 18th and early 19th centuries, the Allegheny, Monongahela, and upper Ohio Rivers became part of a great system of American commercial waterways carrying people and goods to river ports and the world as the nation expanded to the northwest and the southwest.

By 1786, dense forests of the best kinds of timber and water-powered sawmills supported a boat-building industry of vast proportions. In 1819, the National Road (present-day US Route 40) was completed to Brownsville in western Pennsylvania. However, the need for transportation more economical than overland trails and roads generated intense interest in waterway improvements.

To protect navigation along the river system, state governments declared most streams to be navigable public highways, requiring that navigation along them not be obstructed. But permanent improvements to navigation on the Monongahela were beyond the technological and financial resources of local and state governments. Such improvements awaited the greater expertise and resources available to the United States Army Corps of Engineers during the later half of the 19th and early half of the 20th centuries.

Modern-day battles over pollution were just emerging as industrialization brought increasing tension between advocates of economic development and environmental preservation.

SCENE 2: A NATION GROWING

Cast:

Thomas Branson, Joshua Branson's heir and leader in the commercial and community lives of the City of Monongahela Inlet.

Samuel Branson, Thomas Branson's son, a veteran of the Confederate States Army who served in West Virginia, Kentucky and Tennessee. Samuel was wounded several times and limps.

Joshua McKenzie, Thom McKenzie's heir and leader in the industrial and community lives of the City of Monongahela Inlet.

Lemuel McKenzie, Joshua McKenzie's son, a veteran of the United States Army who served in West Virginia, Kentucky, and Tennessee. Lemuel was wounded during the Battle of Chickamauga.

Samuel and Lemuel are lifelong friends who parted for the duration of their service in the Civil War and returned to their homes and rekindled their close friendship. Both campaigned in present-day West Virginia during the winter of 1861–1862, and fought in battles in Kentucky and Tennessee during 1862 and 1863, receiving wounds in 1863 that removed them from the war. While present on or near the same battlefields, they did not knowingly face each other, though they thought often about the possibility.

Sam and Lem are becoming leading citizens of Monongahela Inlet, focusing on business affairs. Conflict arises as issues regarding community sustainability, industrialization, and preservation of the environment emerge.

Belle Branson, Thomas Branson's wife, who minds the store while Thomas and Samuel manage the family's farm and commercial interests.

Sara McKenzie, Lemuel McKenzie's wife, who teaches school while Joshua and Lemuel manage the family's industrial interests.

Feona Dalton, widow of Nathan Dalton and now proprietor of their Monongahela Inlet Inn.

James Dalton, Feona's son and apprentice to the telegraph operator in McKenzie's freight office.

Setting:

With the Bransons, Feona is joint owner of the restaurant that serves the Inn and is located next to the Bransons' store, the two being separated by a wall with large swinging doors. The restaurant is a local gathering place, with people constantly dropping in for coffee, tea, and conversation as well as meals. Presently, Thomas, Samuel, Joshua, and Lemuel are seated at a table in the restaurant and are being served coffee by Feona.

▪ ▪ ▪

FEONA. More coffee, boys?

JOSHUA. No thanks, Feona. We're about finished here. Sam, Lem, the years since our grandfathers settled this town have been good to us. The boatyard is surrounded by machine shops, forges, and a plant that produces steamboat boilers. With timber and coal from our mountains, we are nearly self-sufficient in our manufactories. Hundreds, perhaps thousands, of men are employed as far north as Pittsburgh and up the Allegheny where industry and commerce have flourished. The boatyards and mills along the

Monongahela have played a big part in the war and in the way west.

THOMAS. And the farms and timber operations help to sustain our river communities and furnish food and lumber for the war effort. The McKenzie Freight Line keeps us in touch with folks back East, moving our goods to the railroad stations and when the Monongahela is at low flow. After the war, we'll clear the snags from the river, and build more boats and barges. The National Road and the Baltimore and Ohio Rail Road tie us both east and west with the growth of the nation. Old Joshua Branson said many years ago that we would be the heart of this country, and his vision has become truth.

SAM. That railroad . . . I remember when Jones and Imboden brought the boys north to try to cut that road in '63, and old Stonewall held Harpers Ferry a bit before that.

LEM. But, even as much as they and Lee and Jackson could bring to bear, the Monongahela and the B&O remained stalwart arteries in the heart of the Union.

With a burst of energy, young James Dalton rushes into the room.

JAMES. It's over! It's over! Lee and Grant signed at Appomattox Courthouse, and Johnston surrendered to Sherman in Carolina.

Sam and Lem look at each other, relief and joy showing on their faces, then stand and shake hands. Belle Branson enters from the store and embraces Sam and Lem together. Joshua and Thomas shake hands. Feona hugs her son, James.

JOSHUA. Well, Thomas, now we can get on with the

business of building up this town. Tomorrow, let's talk about the future of Monongahela Inlet.

THOMAS. Right now, we'd better get back to work.

All but Feona and James leave. The lights grow dim, then brighten as Joshua, Thomas, Samuel, Lemuel, Belle, and Sara enter the restaurant and are greeted by Feona.

FEONA. Welcome, all. Coffee's hot, buttermilk is cool, and bacon and eggs are ready for the pan. I'm looking forward to what you see as the future for our fair city.

JOSHUA. Now, Feona, don't get yourself too excited about what's in our heads.

SARA. Don't pay attention to that fluff, Feona. Josh has hardly stopped talking about "the future of Monongahela Inlet" since he came home yesterday.

BELLE. And I've enjoyed the aroma of your coffee and bacon since we opened the store this morning, so I'm ready to fill a cup and a plate and call this meeting to order. Sam, Lem, seat yourselves right now, and you old men stop hemming and hawing around.

All seat themselves as Feona moves around serving coffee and biscuits.

SAMUEL. Lem and I have been talking, too. We've seen the bounty of this land at work for good and ill. Our logging and farming enterprise match almost any in the land. But, the land is wearing hard where we clear the forest and cut on the steep slopes. And the river is looking pretty yellow where the mines drain and we dump the waste from our mills and factories. Up and down the river and its tributaries, where drilling for oil is taking place, a black tarry substance is floating on the water and fouling the river banks.

LEMUEL. That is the price of progress and keeping our businesses competitive. Though smaller than those of Pittsburgh, our manufactories are their equal in quality, and we produce as much man for man as they do. If we don't advance our enterprise as fast as we can, others will overtake us and we will fail to sustain our place along the river.

SAMUEL. If we damage our land and waters, we may not be able to sustain ourselves in any event.

SARA. We need to improve our school if we are to ensure that our young people will grow into able workers and citizens.

BELLE. We won't be able to keep up our stores and schools or anything else if our enterprise fails to produce and sustain good jobs. We're going to be hard pressed to find work for the soldiers coming home from the war, and I fear that many of our sons and daughters will head west or for the big cities.

Thomas and Joshua have been quietly listening to the others bring up their varied points of interest.

JOSHUA. All my life, I have advanced the interests of our manufactories, often with little regard for the consequences to the land and water.

THOMAS. As have I, Joshua, in my zeal to expand our commerce and agriculture.

JOSHUA. It is time, I think, for us to use the talents we have spent developing Monongahela Inlet to examine the issues Sam and Lem, and Sara and Belle, have brought to this table.

THOMAS. We have built soundly upon our past. Now, we must look with that same earnestness at what we have wrought and what the future holds in store.

JOSHUA. Thomas McKenzie and Joshua Branson settled this inlet, creek, and river shore, and set in motion all we see before us. They believed that nature's bounty would last forever; but, more and more, I think *we* must secure that bounty with *our* actions, now and in the future.

THOMAS. This is our land to make of it what we will. We can do nearly anything we like, though later we may not like what we have done. Let us resolve, therefore, to do wisely.

End Scene 2

NARRATION 3

c. 1850–1950

The decades between the mid-19th and mid-20th centuries saw great change in the United States. The American Civil War challenged the survival of the nation, and steamboats were used extensively in the war effort on the Mississippi, Ohio, Cumberland, and Tennessee Rivers. The population grew and filled the sparsely settled West. Advancing technology brought manufacturing to communities across the continent. Throughout the period, the Monongahela River Valley economy grew with the country, and contributed to a changing world as well.

During the first half of the 20th century, the United States was engaged in two world wars. Pittsburgh's three rivers region became known as the Arsenal of Democracy. And not only the tools of war, but countless products useful to a growing nation were mined, milled, and manufactured along and transported upon the rivers. At one time, the Monongahela River carried more tons of materials and manufactures than any other waterway in the world.

Among the consequences of community and economic development in the Monongahela River watershed was environmental degradation. Air and water quality were threatened, and river flora and fauna were submitted to great stress. Waste disposal and water treatment costs increased, and financial stress for both private and public enterprise increased as well. Conflict between those advocating preservation of the natural environment and those promoting community and economic development led to governmental regulation, public involvement in private-sector decision-making, and battles in local, state, and federal courts.

SCENE 3: A NATION DEFENDED

Cast:

Bradley McKenzie, boat builder and coal dock operator.

McKenzie Jordon, captain of the towboat *Branson Belle*, and Brad McKenzie's grandson.

Samantha Branson, wildlife biologist, Department of Natural Resources (DNR), and Celia Branson's daughter.

Celia Branson, owner of the River Front Café.

Mattie Matherson, editor of the local newspaper, the *Monongahela Daily Journal*.

Jenny Forester, retired history professor and president of the local historical society.

Jarvis Stedman, coal operator.

Setting:

The River Front Café, built in 1935 at the site of the restaurant and inn founded by Joshua Branson near the close of the 18th century, continues to provide a center for coffee, tea, and conversation on the waterfront of Monongahela Inlet. The time is the mid-20th century, c. 1955, after World War II and the Korean Conflict. It is a time of community stress after the highly charged wartime effort and before the change in industrial activity along the river. The scene opens with McKenzie Jordon entering the café to see Mattie Matherson and Jenny Forester seated with Celia Branson, enjoying mid-morning coffee and small talk before the busy lunch trade comes to the café.

■　■　■

CELIA. Mornin', Captain. Care to join this august and witty crew?

MCKENZIE. I can hardly imagine a more delightful prospect. Mornin', Mattie, Jenny, Celia.

MATTIE. Up the river or down this trip, Mac?

MCKENZIE. Downriver, Mattie . . . picking up a six-barge tow of Jarvis Stedman's coal at Dad's dock and moving it to the Littleford Point power plant.

JENNY. With more and more air conditioning being installed in buildings these days, Littleford will be generating electricity 'round the clock.

MATTIE. Word among the editors is that AC for homes will be the next big push.

CELIA. I'm talking with Jake Borden about installing AC in the café. He thinks it's just a matter of time until restaurants, stores, and offices will be air conditioned, and when folks get used to it there, they will want it at home.

McKENZIE. Celia, do you expect to see Sam today?

CELIA. Yeah, she's been working on water quality in the Monongahela and some of the tributaries.

MATTIE. The wire services are sending us feature articles about pollution problems in the rivers and bay areas surrounded by heavy mining and manufacturing activity. Some are saying that the fertilizers and bug killers that help us keep food on our tables and feed much of the world are a mixed blessing as well. Sam told me recently that silting in the runs and creeks where mining, logging, and gas-well drilling has expanded may be causing loss of fish habitat in addition to the chemical problems.

CELIA, *with a chuckle*. Old Andy Kilpatrick is forever complaining about losing his favorite fishing holes.

JENNY. We may be running out of the historical "dilution is the solution to pollution" response to our changing world. There seems to be a growing concern with water purification and sewage disposal, and whether cities are going to be required to build expensive plants to treat the river water we drink and the sewage we put into our rivers.

CELIA. Jake goes on and on about trash dumps and landfills, and the garbage and trash pick-up charges for the café are expected to go up pretty soon.

McKENZIE. I see yellow in the tributaries flowing into the Mon every day, and occasional oil slicks. But, the river has been our main highway for a long time, and it is still the cheapest way to transport coal, limestone, sand and gravel, and a lot of other things that are heavy or bulky. A few weeks ago, I brought a barge upriver that carried a gigantic machine that couldn't be shipped by truck or train; it was going into one of the power plants along the river. The river is a superhighway of vast proportions.

JENNY. It proved its worth during two world wars and as far back as the French and Indian War when we shipped timber, built boats and barges, manufactured iron and steel and chemicals, even blue-ocean war ships that were moved downriver to the Gulf of Mexico and the seven seas. The history of industry, commerce, and life along the Monongahela River is rich, and we are richer for it.

The door opens, and Samantha Branson enters energetically.

SAMANTHA. Wow, is this ever a serious looking outfit!

McKenzie Jordon leaps to his feet and turns toward Samantha.

SAMANTHA. It's really good to see you Mac. You've been on the river the last couple of times I've dropped in here. (*Hugging Celia and looking at the others.*) And a hearty hi-ho to the rest of you.

CELIA. You've come just in time to join our pontificating about your favorite subject: the Monongahela River.

SAM, *glancing at McKenzie*. Well, I do have *some* interests in addition to rivers and wildlife. What's up?

JENNY. We're waxing eloquently about the problems and promises of the mighty Monongahela, how we've benefited from and abused her down through the years, and what she might have in store for us. I'm sure you'll have *some* interest in the topic.

SAM. I absolutely do. But, at this very minute, I want hot coffee and warm apple pie. Please continue while I return to civilization from the cold, often inhospitable, life of the wild world scientist.

Bradley McKenzie and Jarvis Stedman enter the café just as Celia sets pie and coffee in front of Samantha.

JARVIS. Looks like quite a party, Brad, and we're just in time for pie and coffee.

BRAD. Maybe after lunch, Jarvis. Good morning, ladies. Mac, we'll have all the barges loaded in time for you to make Littleford Point before dark, that is if you aren't too far back in the queues at the locks.

JARVIS. Must be a heavy-weight conversation from the serious looks on your faces. Couldn't be another of your "dilution is no longer the pollution solution" could it, Jenny?

JENNY. Jarvis, you'd be downright disappointed if it weren't, and you've arrived just in time to hear from the "wild world scientist."

JARVIS. I'm always glad to hear what Sam has to say, but any way you cut it, this town and, by golly, this nation need our coal as much now as during the war. Jobs and paychecks, steel and electricity . . . Why, just this morning, Brad and I attended a meeting with folks from Littleford aimed at increasing the amount of coal shipping to the plant so they can generate more electricity for economic development. We've got a lot of shaky businesses up and down the river, and wrestling with a bunch of new rules and regulations isn't helping much.

MATTIE. Is this for publication, Jarvis? I always spell your name right, even when I'm printing the same message for the umpteenth time.

All laugh, including Jarvis. Smiling, Jarvis replies.

JARVIS. By golly, Mattie, you don't miss a beat. I doubt if any of your readers are unsure of my thoughts on the subject, or of my concern for the costs of complying with the regulations being discussed in legislatures along the river and in Washington, DC.

BRAD. And the impact of those costs on the price of coal at our mills and power plants, and the competitiveness of our coal in world markets. Though regulations at home may affect all of us the same, they won't apply overseas, and patchworking regs from state to state will pit us against each other and the foreign producers. We've got to move real carefully on this.

JENNY. Historically, improving technology has helped us work out some solutions *and* stay competitive. All of it *is* costly, though, and that includes ensuring that we keep our water, air, and people safe and healthy.

MATTIE. Our readers are aware of the threat to their jobs and communities and appear to be awakening to the issues of polluting our water, air, and lands. But, it is hard to get agreement on what to do about it.

SAMANTHA. In the 18th century, when he and Joshua Branson settled here and laid the foundation for this city, Thom McKenzie thought the bounty of this land would last forever. We know now that this land and this river have suffered, even as they have sustained us through two centuries. We aren't real sure how much more of *us* they can take, but we're pretty sure that if we do our part, they can take care of us far into the future . . . if only we will.

End Scene 3

NARRATION 4: CONCLUSION AND CHALLENGE: LIFE ON AND ALONG THE MONONGAHELA RIVER, C. 1950–2050

The narrator steps into the light to challenge the audience to discover what has happened on and along the river since mid-20th century and to imagine what will happen between now and the middle of the 21st century.

The 18th, 19th and 20th centuries witnessed the development of the United States of America. Spanning the continent of North America from the Atlantic to the Pacific, the USA became a colossus playing on a world stage. Near its center lies one of the world's great inland waterways, the Mississippi River, the eastern reach of which is comprised of the Ohio River watershed with its two great tributaries, the Allegheny and the Monongahela.

Since the middle of the 20th century, river traffic along the Monongahela has changed. Commercial shipping has declined and recreational boating has surged. The dams and locks that sustained navigation for more than a century and a half have aged, and the resources to maintain them appear inadequate. Communities along its banks have changed as well.

Conflict between environmental preservation and industrial development continues unabated. The apparently disparate viewpoints are encased in wide-ranging arguments presented in public meetings, legislative deliberations, permitting processes, and other venues throughout the Monongahela watershed and the states that encompass it. Economic development, water quality, air pollution, brownfields, community transition, public health, wildlife habitat, jobs, electric power grids, mountaintop mining, drilling in the Marcellus

shale, rural roads—all and more are issues that con-
front us daily.

What might we expect during the first half of the
21st century? Who will profit; who will pay? *What do
you think the future holds for us?*

THE END

PARLOR GAMES

Synopsis:
A one-act, three-scene play about the unintended consequences of gossip, *Parlor Games* dramatizes the common parlor game in which a brief message is passed
from player to player, changing as it flows along the
way, and ending differently than it began.

Cast:
Andy
Celia
Zach, Celia's estranged husband
Annalise, Andy's sister and co-owner of Anna-Belle's
    Beauty Parlor
Isabelle, Annalise's partner in Anna-Belle's Beauty Parlor
The phone chain:
Billie
Mabel
Izy
Trish
Mona
Trev, Mona's husband and Zach's brother

Setting:

A small town in rural Appalachia.

SCENE 1

Anna-Belle's Beauty Parlor. Annalise and Isabelle, co-owners of the parlor, each at work with a patron.

ISABELLE. How is Andy doing these days, Ann? I haven't seen him since he was here a little while after your momma died.

ANNALISE. Good, Belle. He came into town earlier this morning to deliver some stuff from the Trafalgar County Sheriff to the District State Police Office; "unbroken chain of evidence" or some such police talk. He's over at the house now going through Momma's papers and the stuff he left behind when he went to the war three years ago. Momma kept everything in pretty good order, but there's still lots to deal with, and we gotta decide where we go from here. Later today, he's stopping by the shop.

ISABELLE. I loved your momma, Ann. Her and old Andy Jack were the Momma and Daddy I never had.

ANNALISE. Belle, she was ready to go. I remember almost every word she said to me and Doc Prentise that night. "This may be a night for tears, but before this night passes, I'll be sittin' at the feet of Jesus at the right hand of the Lord with Andy Jack's hand in mine. So don't you fret none, this'll be all right." Near broke Andy's heart, though. He was in that field hospital so far away and didn't know anything about Momma's passin' 'til the funeral and all was over. By then, it was near time for him to come home, so he just waited 'til his tour in Afghanistan was up. He's been a deputy sheriff in Trafalgar County since he got out of the Army MPs.

ISABELLE. It's tough to be so far away when a thing like that happens. My schedule is full for the day, Ann. Can you take any more today?

ANNALISE. I have only one more appointment. Celia will be in later.

BILLIE, *sitting in Annalise's chair.* How is Celia doing these days, what with her breakup with Zach and all?

ANNALISE. She's doing better, Billie, now that she and Zach aren't together. Life with Zach had got pretty rough, and he still hangs on to her.

BILLIE. I never did think much of that match. I know Zach was hurt real bad when him and Andy got blown up. But when he come home with his disability and all, Celia saved him by making him go to the VA counseling. Don't s'pose, though, that she'd married him if Andy had been here. Poor Celia got the worst of that deal.

ANNALISE. It's time for the dryer, Billie.

Billie moves into a chair under the hair dryer. Annalise lowers the dryer over Billie's head, and turns on the dryer.

BILLIE, *takes out her cell phone and begins texting a message and speaking out loud.* Mabel, you'll never believe what I just heard . . .

End Scene 1

SCENE 2

Stage dark. Two spotlights show ladies seated talking on cell phones.

IZY. Did you say Andy Stoddard will be in Anna-Belle's later today?

MABEL. That's what Billie said.

IZY. And Celia has an appointment this afternoon *at the same time*?

MABEL. Yep.

IZY. My God, Mabel. If Zach finds out Andy has come back to see Celia after he told him to stay away from her, they'll be the devil to pay! Better keep this under our hats. Oops, I got another call coming in, so I gotta go.

Stage dark. Two spotlights show Izy and Trish seated talking on cell phones.

IZY. I know it sounds crazy, Trish, but, that's what Mabel said. If Zach finds Celia with Andy Stoddard . . . well, who knows what'll happen. Mabel doesn't always get things right, but why would Andy come back to town just now? It ain't like he shows up every other day, you know? Andy and Celia was pretty friendly before him and Zach went to Afghanistan.

TRISH. Them three was great friends growing up, Izy, but three's a crowd, ya know. They ain't been close since Andy and Zach come back from the war. Now that Andy is a deputy over in Trafalgar County, he's pretty much been out of the picture. But if he's got wind of the breakup and has come back to take up with Celia . . . well, who knows what Zach'll do. Keep me posted, OK? I'll let Mona know we're playing bridge at your house this week.

Stage dark. Two spotlights show Trisha and Mona seated talking on cell phones.

TRISH. Mona, you haven't been around here long enough to know how it was with Celia, Zach, and Andy before Zach and Celia got married. Andy and Celia had got pretty close before them boys went to the war. It ain't good for Andy to come after Celia right now. Before I forget, we're playing at Izy's house Thursday. Maybe Celia'll have something to tell us then.

MONA. It ain't like Celia to treat Zach like that, Trish. And I thought Andy knows how Zach feels about him and Celia.

TRISH. I ain't exactly saying Andy come back to see Celia. But, it is quite a coincidence, don't you think?

Trev enters Mona's spotlight.

MONA. Gotta go, Trish. Trev just came home. I'll see you Thursday.

Trish's spotlight turns off. Mona holds her phone in her hand.

TREV. Who you gossipin' with now, Mona? Did I hear you say something about Andy Stoddard?

MONA. It's just Trish. You can't hardly believe a word she says.

TREV. What'd Trish say, Mona, that you can't hardly believe?

MONA. It's just gossip, Trev. You know how those ladies are. They can't pass a day without some sort of shenanigans going on.

TREV. What "shenanigans?"

MONA. Just girl talk, Trev.

TREV. What shenanigans, Mona?

MONA. Well, Izy told Trish that Andy's going to Anna-Belle's to see Annalise this afternoon.

TREV. And what else, Mona?

MONA. Nothing, Trev.

TREV. Mona, what else?

MONA, *Pause.* Celia has an appointment with Ann this afternoon.

TREV. Hell, Mona! If Zach hears about this . . . give me the phone!

MONA. Oh God, Trev, don't call Zach! You know how he feels about Andy and Celia.

TREV. Give me the damn phone, Mona!

MONA, *hands the phone to Trev.* Please, Trev, you know how Zach is.

TREV, *dials the phone.* Yeah, Mona, but he's got a right to know.

TREV, *speaks into the phone.* Zach, where're you at?

In background: engine sounds; country music as if from a car radio.

ZACH, *off stage and in a relaxed voice.* Hey Trev, I been up to the VA, and I'm just coming into town. What's up?

TREV. Zach, Andy Stoddard's in town! He's hooking up with Celia this afternoon at Anna-Belle's.

Silence.

MONA. Trev, I didn't say Andy come back to "hook up" with Celia. This could undo all the good that's come of Zach's VA counseling.

ZACH, *growing angrier.* I knew Celia wished she'd waited for Andy Stoddard, and I told that son-of-a-bitch what I'd do if he come back to see her.

TREV. Cool it, Zach. You know Andy's a deputy over in Trafalgar County, and that cowboy sheriff makes his deputies pack their badges and guns 24/7.

Silence.

ZACH, *bitter and tense.* I told him.

The call ends.

TREV. Zach, Zach . . . *Trev turns to Mona.* He hung up.

MONA. Call him back, Trev, and set him straight.

TREV, *dials then listens.* He ain't answerin'.

MONA, *walks out of the light.* I'm going to Anna-Belle's. Maybe I can catch Zach before he does something foolish.

End Scene 2

SCENE 3

In Anna-Belle's: Celia is in the hairdresser's chair; Annalise is working with her hair. Isabelle is working with another patron.

ANDY, *enters the beauty shop.* Hi, Ann . . . Isabelle.

ISABELLE, *smiles at Andy.* Long time, no see, Andy.

ANNALISE. Hi. Did you find all your stuff at Momma's?

ANDY. Most of it, I think. I put it in Mom's flowery luggage; it's in the car.

Annalise turns the chair until Celia is facing Andy.

CELIA. I always loved that luggage. Your mom told me where she got it, and I bought the same bags to take on my honeymoon when I married Zach. Hi, Andy.

Celia rises from the chair and kisses Andy on the cheek.

ZACH, *bursts into the shop and sees Celia with Andy.* I told you to stay away from Celia, Andy; damn it, I told you.

ANNALISE. Wait, Zach. Andy's just here to get some of his stuff from Momma's house.

ZACH. Bull shit, Ann. Trev told me why Andy and Celia are here.

CELIA. What are you talking about, Zach?

ZACH. Mona told Trev you two are clearing out together!

ANDY. Hold on a minute, Zach.

ZACH. Shut your mouth, Andy Stoddard! You ain't got nothin' to say I wanna hear!

CELIA. That's all wrong, Zach!

ZACH. Don't lie to me, Celia. I saw the suitcases you got for our honeymoon in the back seat of Andy's car.

ANNALISE. Those are Momma's bags, Zach.

ZACH. Your little brother can't hide behind you no more, Ann.

ANDY. Come on, Zach. This ain't the way to work things out.

ZACH, *draws a gun from his belt and points it at Andy.* Shut up, Andy! Shut up!

CELIA, *walks toward Zach with her arms extended.* It ain't the way you're sayin', Zach.

ZACH, *jabs the gun violently toward Celia and yells.* You lyin' bi—

BANG! The bullet slams into Celia's chest, rocking her backward into Andy's arms.

Zach, eyes widening in horror, steps back, stares at the spreading red spot over Celia's heart, then raises his hands to his head as if in pain, moans, turns, and stumbles through the door, crashing into Mona, knocking her to the floor. Andy catches Celia and slowly lowers her toward the floor. As Celia's body lowers, the lights dim. Andy kneels holding Celia in his arms. A single gunshot sounds off-stage where Zach exited, and the lights go out.

EPILOGUE

On the side of the stage opposite Zach's exit, a single spotlight illuminates Billie sitting in a chair and speaking into her cell phone.

BILLIE. Mabel, how in God's name do such things happen?

THE END

ESSAYS

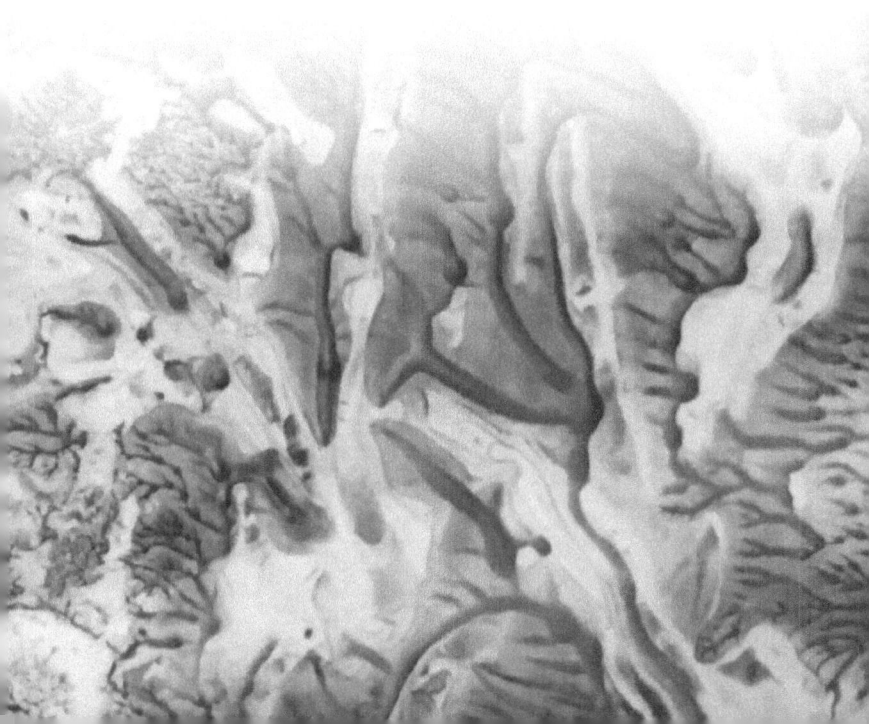

AUTHOR'S NOTE

THE 20TH CENTURY AS VIEWED FROM THE 21ST

TO FRAME THE ESSAYS, a few highlights of the last century: Commencing before the turn to the 20th century, worldwide industrialization, reality-based political philosophies (anarchism, capitalism, colonialism, communism, imperialism, nationalism, socialism), "robber barons" and progressive reformers, war in Cuba and the Philippines, incursion into northern Mexico in pursuit of Pancho Villa, World War I, the Russian Revolution, the Roaring Twenties, the worldwide economic depression of the 1930s, George Orwell's battlefield experience during Spain's civil war, World War II, the atomic bomb, the victory of Communism in China, Orwell's 1984 (published in 1949), armed conflicts— wars in all but name—in Korea and Vietnam reflecting the division of the World War II alliance into disparate armed camps fostered respectively by the USA/NATO and the USSR/PRC during a Cold War that festered for half a century then appeared to disappear before, arguably, reemerging after the turn to the 21st century.

In the United States, economically, politically and socially, the century spanned the era from the Gilded

Age to the Golden Parachute. Both turns of the century similarly featured international strife, significant differences between wealth and poverty, and adverse economic pressures on the common peoples. Norman Mailer, considered by some to have been the innovator of creative nonfiction, said of the 20th century, "The horror of the Twentieth Century was the size of each new event, and the paucity of its reverberation."

The essays examine legacies of the 20th century from three viewpoints. The first essay is a view from the 21st century through a lens fashioned from George Orwell's classic dystopian novel, 1984. The second essay suggests the value to be found in fiction when encountering uncertainties and chaos in a highly charged, rapidly changing world. The final essay is personal—an aging man reaching for memories of a seven-year-old child watching his father and others go to war and much later be pronounced the "Greatest Generation" —an appellation that, though well-meant, may fall short, given the realities that defined it.

REPRISING ORWELL IN THE 21ST CENTURY

GEORGE ORWELL MAY HAVE GOT IT RIGHT when he wrote at the end of his mid-20th-century dystopian novel, *1984*, "It was chiefly to allow time for the preliminary work of translation that the final adoption of Newspeak had been fixed for so late a date as 2050." Could it be that Orwell's vision was more prescient than readers then and now were aware, that the fiction published in 1949 contained glimpses of the real world advancing upon us today?

Bridging from Orwell to today, William Lutz opened the preface to his 1989 book, *Doublespeak*, with this from Orwell: "Most people who bother with the matter at all would admit that the English language is in a bad way." Lutz followed, however, with: "The English language is doing quite well, thank you; it is we who use the English language who are not doing well, not doing well at all."

Three decades before 2050, we have gravitated from the First Amendment to the US Constitution to the contemporary terms "politically correct," "coddling of the American mind," "post-truth," and "alternate facts." Indeed, "post-truth" was named 2016 "Word of the

Year" by the England-based *Oxford English Dictionary*, topping *Merriam-Webster's* suggestion, "fascism." The word I seem to hear most often and find most disturbing, however, is the simple four-letter word, "hate."

In the introduction to Greg Lukianoff and Jonathan Haidt's article "The Coddling of the American Mind" (September 2015), the editors of the *Atlantic* wrote: "College students are increasingly demanding protection from words and ideas they don't like and seeking punishment of those who give even accidental offense." Haley Edwards, in her December 14, 2015, article in *Time*, "The Fallacy of Free Speech," describes the rhetoric of an aspirant to the US presidency as, "to jettison intellectual engagement in favor of an emotional response, to prize feelings over reason, to intimidate, rather than engage with, those who would disagree." The cover of Lee McIntyre's 2018 book, *Post-Truth*, sums up the book's theme: "How we arrived in the post-truth era, when 'alternative facts' replace actual facts, and feelings have more weight than evidence." McIntyre begins the book with this from Orwell: "The very concept of objective truth is fading out of the world. Lies will pass into history."

In addition to "Newspeak," are there other aspects of protagonist Winston Smith's Orwellian world that might ring a contemporary bell?

OCEANIA, EURASIA, AND EASTASIA

The US Monroe Doctrine, North Atlantic Treaty Organization, East Asian military alliances, and international trade systems such as Bretton Woods, NAFTA, TPP, and European trade proposals bear a resemblance to Orwell's Oceania and its continual war with either Eurasia or Eastasia. The simile is reinforced currently by Russia's actions to secure its interests on its periphery and China's extensions into the South China Sea, South Asia, East Africa, and Latin America.

Today, the United States appears in continuous unarmed conflict with both Russia and China after half a century of cold war; a three-year hot war in Korea from 1950 to 1953 against North Korea and Communist China (to this day, no peace treaty has been concluded); a hot war in Vietnam from 1961 until 1975, resulting in civil strife in America and North Vietnamese victory over South Vietnam and its allies, including at one time more than a half-million US boots on the ground. NATO has extended into east European countries formerly part of the Soviet Bloc. China is blossoming into an economic giant. The reprise of Oceania, Eurasia, and Eastasia?

We might think of Russia as the modern Eurasia, China the modern Eastasia, and the Western Alliance the modern Oceania. NATO may appear to Russia to be hemming in Russia militarily and with economic sanctions, while the United States is allying with several Southeast Asian nations to threaten Chinese interests over large expanses of the South China Sea, interests perhaps analogous to US hegemony over the Gulf of Mexico and the Caribbean Sea. Multiple military alliance systems and international trade agreements and proposals might be construed as directed toward keeping Oceania safe and dominant beyond the Western Hemisphere.

Russian memory extends to the Russo–Japanese War in the first decade of the 20th century (including a surprise Sunday morning attack by the Japanese in 1904 upon the Russian fleet at Port Arthur), intervention by the UK and the USA into the civil war for control in Russia following World War I and battling Germany in World Wars I and II.

Communist China easily recalls fighting Japan in China in the late 1930s and during World War II, civil war with American-supported Chinese Nationalists, and combat with Americans and South Koreans in North Korea during the Korean Conflict.

Western alignments today, apparently aimed at containing Russia and China, include Germany and Japan, both believed to be responsible for 20th-century wars during which Eurasia and Eastasia were brutally attacked.

Post–World War II returns to colonialism coupled with national Communism (misconstrued in the West as monolithic international Stalinism dictated from Moscow) may be remembered in Southeast Asia and Africa as opposition to national freedom from colonial overlords. Tactical operations and strategies in pursuit of freedom often are lost on some but easily recalled by those being trampled while the elephants negotiate in state-supported luxury in Washington, London, and Paris.

OCEANIA'S SOCIAL STRUCTURE—INNER PARTY, OUTER PARTY, AND PROLES (PROLETARIAT)

Current US upper, middle, and lower classes, as well as national and worldwide "haves and have-nots," are topics of continuous political and economic conflict in our daily news.

Orwell's Oceania has four principal demographic levels: Big Brother, who appears everywhere but does not materialize; the Inner Party, approximately 2 percent of the population who rule Oceania; the Outer Party, about 13 percent of the population who carry out the dictates of the party rulers; and the Proles (Proletariat), nearly 85 percent of the population, who simply survive from day to day but do not share in the benefits of party membership.

In governance, some (including more than one US president) have warned about the influence of the military-industrial complex and lobbyists and think tanks financed by corporate interests and wealthy individuals, and the dehumanizing effects of confusing or contradictory laws and rules buried in bureaucracies. Do they represent an inner party served by an outer party comprised of professional administrators and narrowly focused specialists?

While the United States is defined by many as a classless society within which one may rise from lower to middle to upper class based on talent, merit, and hard work, others are rethinking it as a society with classes but not castes. Some have posited that the American middle class is slowly separating into a higher-level middle class and a lower-level middle class based upon education level, employment status, and income of those currently thought of as the broad middle class. Some of the chronic unemployed are being recast as "caste," a relatively permanent underclass who are fated never to rise above their lower-class station—generally owing to age or insufficient education/training—while middle to upper class fluidity remains the face (or myth) presented publicly. Research into the emergence of a more modern and complex class system, conducted in the United Kingdom and later reexamined to correct for recognized bias (The Great British Class Survey, online since 2013), suggests that the traditional working class is changing, the extremes of the class system are very important, and a new and potentially dangerous class—the precariat—has been identified.

Thomas Jefferson thought that generations matter in the sense of governmental imposition of one generation's legacy of laws and rules binding subsequent generations who had no part in formulating the laws and rules that bound them. We are now several generations away from the times that led to George Orwell's and our current states of affairs.

BIG BROTHER AND WINSTON'S TV SET

NSA surveillance, Big Data's analytics, and a recent report by Michael Price, counsel in the Liberty and National Security program at the Brennan Center for Justice at New York University's law school, in which he notes that the privacy statement for his new "smart" TV indicates that it is set to record information about viewed content, facial recognition, and voice recognition, and also includes the warning, "Please be aware that if your spoken words include personal or other sensitive information, that information will be among the data captured and transmitted to a third party." The *New York Times*, the *Atlantic,* and others have reported that DNA databases created for genealogical research by public participants to trace their ancestry have been used by law enforcement agencies, with and without warrants, to augment criminal and victim identification investigations (the DNA-match participants for one such service are told in the search organization's site policy that ". . . participants understand the possible uses of DNA, including the identification of relatives who have committed crimes or were victims of crimes . . ."). Science reporters Gina Kolata and Heather Murphy, writing about the capture of a criminal through finding DNA profiles of his relatives in an ancestry database, note, "Coming so quickly on the heels of the Cambridge Analytica scandal . . . it is beginning to dawn on consumers that even their most intimate digital data—their genetic profiles— may be passed around in ways they never intended." ("The Golden State Killer Is Tracked Through a Thicket of DNA, and Experts Shudder," the *New York Times*, August 27, 2018.) And some federal authorities have requested that computer encrypted documents include "backdoors" that will allow access to the clear text by appropriate federal authorities.

An increasing array of devices, including voice-activated devices that respond to requests for information and music, demonstrate the potential for sensing conditions in homes and private automobiles, keeping track of the locations and operations of commercial vehicles, and monitoring and controling the environment in "private" spaces in homes—voluntarily, of course, as people gravitate toward convenience and personal gratification. For example, Haley Edwards, in her "Alexa Takes the Stand: Listening Devices Raise Privacy Issues," discusses the use in criminal justice of the "third-party doctrine" to introduce "recordings from "artificial intelligence–powered devices such as Google's Home or Samsung's smart TV . . . as evidence in court." (*Time*, May 17, 2017.) And the reconstruction of events and searches for aberrant behavior in public spaces monitored legitimately by surveillance cameras and social media have been demonstrated repeatedly. Recall, for example, the search for terrorist suspects following bomb explosions during the 2013 Boston Marathon.

Cybersecurity is an increasingly troublesome dilemma. Hacking and identity theft have become common topics for our evening news and, for many, crushing personal afflictions. State and non-state incursions into public- and private-sector computer controls and databases regularly challenge our security professionals, yet we continue to plunge headlong into deeper and more critical cyber applications as though they were invulnerable. In 2016, *Time* named "The Hackers" a runner-up for "Person of the Year" in an article subtitled, "They made vulnerability the new normal and took aim at democracy itself." (December 19.) The *New York Times* recently reported that security flaws inside nearly all of the world's computers represent a very real threat to the way cloud-computing systems operate. (Cade Metz and Nicole Pelroth, "Researchers Discover Two Major Flaws in the World's Computers," January 3, 2018.) National security, power grids, personal financial and health information—the list of vulnerabilities we create seems endless and beyond our defensive capabilities.

In graduate school, we would quip: "Do you know the difference between mechanical engineers and civil engineers? Mechanical engineers design weapons and civil engineers design targets." Today, computer gurus design targets, computer hackers design and wield weapons, and private and public enterprises put the targets in play (legally or illegitimately) while achieving only limited success in protecting their—and our—information.

CONCLUSION

The 20th century, for the United States and significant portions of the world, was conceived and born into war and industrial and civil strife. It continued through bouts of all three, interspersed with significant periods of prosperity that seemed to suggest that the worst was behind us. But, the 21st century was similarly conceived and born into war and civil and industrial strife. Déjà vu, all over again?

In his 2016 book, *The Deep State: The Fall of Democracy and the Rise of a Shadow Government*, Mike Lofgren writes, "By the first decade of the 21st century, the Gilded Age had returned." (In their 1873 novel, *The Gilded Age*, Mark Twain and Charles Dudley Warner referred to the Gilded Age as glittering on the surface but corrupt underneath.)

As our world becomes more complex, we are nearly overrun by information and change, some of which seems to represent more style than substance. Making sense of it may be outstripping our human sensibilities. McIntyre says, in closing chapter four of *Post-Truth*, "The challenge to reality is complete." Perhaps by the time 2050 rolls around, we will have completed the translation and final adoption—or rejection—of

Newspeak and will be more respectful of fiction as a tool for examining the essence of reality.

FICTION ILLUMINATING FACT
A PERSONAL POINT OF VIEW

At-one-ment: variation on "atonement"
(from Dan Brown, The Lost Symbol),
arguably an example of fiction illuminating
information that provides a perspective
on facts—as we know them.

IN A PREFATORY NOTE to his novel *The Lost Symbol*, Dan Brown writes, "All organizations in this novel exist . . . All rituals, science, artwork, and monuments in this novel are real." The references to science reach into the current states of brain science and sub-atomic quanta— our world as we know it reaches from measurable but smaller-than-the-human-eye-can-see levels of sub- atomic particles to a universe not visible from the Earth but observable from the Hubble Space Telescope. Seeing is not always necessary for understanding, but sensing is. James Michener's novels are read almost as much for the historic content as for the fictitious plots and char- acters who carry the narrative from a distant past into the modern world. Tom Clancy's *Search for Red October* is enjoyed by many for the realism he incorporated into his fiction. Michael Crichton's fiction always spins off cutting-edge science. Allan Eckart's series focusing on Native Americans and European colonists in America, though published as historical fiction, is often referred to as narrative history. Indeed, science fiction, historic fiction, and narrative history are prominent and authoritative parts of our literary heritage and current mainstream.

Can we enjoy popular fiction as we explore reality?

Thinking about the future, making plans, is using "fictions" to guide future actions; a plan is using what we know, and can reasonably expect, to peer into the future—to plan, organize, control, and communicate a way from where we are to where we want to be—to travel in time from a place or position we know to a place or position we seek with reasonable hopes for success. Citizens, if they wish to participate in the journey, occasionally must think and argue with their leaders, others, and themselves. To do so, they must create their own "fictions," their own visions of places or positions they seek and their own thoughts about the "facts" not yet in evidence that represent their futures and the ways and means for securing their futures.

Recently, we cast ballots for political leadership extending months and years into our future. Some of us voted with high expectations that our favored candidates could deliver a future that meets our visions. Some of us may have voted with skepticism bordering upon lower expectations of favorable outcomes because the representatives of other viewpoints showed signs of more strength in the political arena. There was a time when we might have exclaimed, "Next time . . ." Now, the schism across our political baseline, the shadowy futures at the extremes of our political realm, are so vast as to threaten the abyss. We wonder at the governance abyss—Democrats and Republicans locked in a win–lose battle between political parties rather than engaged in a win–win contest in service to the nation and its people. We wonder at Islam's abyss—Shia and Sunni, and in earlier Europe, Catholic and Protestant. We wonder at the abyss between Israeli and Palestinian. We wonder whether the Cold War is being reprised on the European stage and whether the Korean peninsula will once again erupt. We wonder whether compromise will be judged as surrender. We wonder whether technology and change are falling so rapidly and hard around us that we can't learn fast enough to keep up. We wonder whether our future is red, blue, or purple. We wonder whether our future is utopian or dystopian.

How do utopias and dystopias differ? Discussing different definitions of genre in her 2017 Great Courses lecture series, *Great Utopian and Dystopian Works of Literature*, Dr. Pamela Bedore, University of Connecticut, states (paraphrased):

> Genre with its recognizable conventions develops in response to specific situations, specific problems or anxieties in the world, and is a way of addressing or responding to that anxiety. Under this framework, utopia and dystopia represent two different rhetorical responses, often to the same anxieties. Utopia is one rhetorical approach: we can solve this problem if we take these certain steps. Dystopia is a different rhetorical approach—it functions as a cautionary tale: don't take these steps or this terrible reality will happen. Utopia presents hope; dystopia, fear.

As examples, I suggest the following books, all fiction:

1. Utopian: Edward Bellamy, *Looking Backward: 2000–1887*, first published in 1888.
2. Dystopian: Jack London, *The Iron Heel*, published in 1908.
3. Dystopian: George Orwell, 1984, published in 1949.

The first two books may seem far out of date. But, because I believe that the passage from the 20th century to the 21st century bears substantive similarities to the passage from the 19th century to the 20th century, I am comfortable recommending reading them today, more than a century after the times, capitalist philosophies, and industrial practices they represent. As Mark Twain is reputed to have opined, "History does not repeat but it does rhyme."

Orwell's works have resurged recently, in part because some elements of his stories appear to be reflected in current events. *1984* and its predecessor *Animal Farm* (1945) are good adult reads, and connections with current events make their satirical commentary interesting and entertaining. They provide special insights into historical events that had a direct bearing on the lives of those of us who experienced life from the mid-20th century into the 21st.

Truthfully, I similarly welcome good movies—both documentary and fictional—to the process by adding sights, sounds, and drama to the intellectual experience. Expecting fiction to employ parable, symbology, metaphor, and allegory to illuminate events, I value fiction as it brings the past, present, and future into the thought process.

Arthur Conan Doyle's Sherlock Holmes adventures exemplify the value of employing fiction in nonfiction books. *Sherlock's Logic* (1986) is a nonfiction book in which the author, William Neblett, ". . . draws the reader into the world of logical deduction by way of . . . a unique and entertaining illustration of the various forms of reasoning, correct and fallacious, deductive and inductive, and a demonstration of how logic is present in everyday life." Daniel Smith gave us *How to Think Like Sherlock* (2013) so we might "learn Holmes's method . . . his system for sorting clues from trivia, truth from lies, and guilt from innocence." In *The Science of Sherlock Holmes* (2006), E. J. Wagner quotes one of the preeminent forensic scientists of the early 20th century as suggesting "that students of forensic science read the Sherlock Holmes tales as examples of proper scientific approach and to obtain a perspective on the new directions forensic science might take." At the end, Wagner offers an appropriate caveat, "He [Doyle] wrote of science but viewed through a storyteller's lens." Thus does fiction enliven nonfiction prose.

Seeking understanding through fiction is not a casual undertaking. Just as skepticism regarding the news of the day helps us challenge and find value in the cacophony of information constantly bombarding us, reading fiction skeptically allows us to glean from the hyperbolic treatment of facts a visceral sense of the realities that they represent. But we must keep in mind that narrative history, historical fiction, and novels often inform us through parable, metaphor, allegory, symbol, myth, legend, opinion, misdirection; often serving up facts in costume leaving us to penetrate the mask to discern the face of reality. At its best, it is interesting, challenging, and entertaining for both reader and writer.

Can we use fiction to explore reality? Yes, but with vital caveats—fiction may be based upon fact, may include fact, may inform as fact; but fiction is not fact though it may be as close to truth as we will ever get. Virginia Woolf: "Fiction is like a spider web, attached ever so slightly perhaps, but still attached to life at all four corners. Often the attachment is scarcely perceptible."

Every day, in a laboratory, workplace, or somewhere, someone's science fiction becomes scientific fact; someone's business plan becomes a business reality; someone's hope leads to a utopia, if only for a while; someone's fear descends into a dystopia, perhaps for far too long; someone striving finds success or failure, until the next time.

I do fear that so long as our political antagonists peer at each other from bunkers on opposite sides of a schism, we will be unable to realize the benefits of our own better natures. I hope we can bridge the abyss before too many of us march self-righteously into it. Good stories can help us understand and undertake the task.

COMING TO KNOW THE GREATEST GENERATION

FOR TWO OF MY THREE BROTHERS AND ME, life began during the Great Depression that preceded World War II. Tom Brokaw's Greatest Generation included our parents and their brothers, sisters, neighbors, and friends. For us, they were the community we grew up in. They were the greatest, but they were not yet the "greatest generation."

One fall morning, we went off to elementary school in the old Normal School building on the campus of Glenville State Teachers College while our mother walked with our father to the small-town Greyhound bus stop where he set off for US Navy basic training, diesel mechanic school at Great Lakes, boat training at San Diego (LCVPs), passage over the International Date Line and the equator on a warship bound upon a "mission of war" delivering live marines to and carrying living, wounded, dying, and dead marines from Pacific islands from New Guinea to Okinawa, and ferrying damage assessment teams upriver to Nagasaki.

We followed his journey on radio and through Movietone News in the theater on Main Street. Mom saved every issue of the *Clarksburg Telegram* until Dad came home long after the blazing red headlines "VE Day" and "VJ Day."

In subsequent years, Glenville State burgeoned with returning veterans, who laughed and cursed like the sailors, soldiers, and airmen they had been, and played football with abandon as only young men who had lived the horrors of war could muster. We got to know many of them because we played on their campus, delivered their daily newspapers, and were taught by them as they completed their student teaching in our classrooms.

For us, my two brothers and me, they were not the "greatest generation." They were our father and mother and countless others whom we admired and longed to become. And they were *giants*.

AFTERWORD

THIS HAS BEEN A JOURNEY along a foggy roadway. Unable to decide upon a single way, I wandered through a world of opportunities, pausing from time to time to experience a few of the joys of one opportunity before setting out for another. Each tomorrow very quickly became a memory; the next tomorrow lay just inside the fog I faced. Much that I did today was in anticipation of a world that lay ahead; much that I knew today was prelude to much I needed to learn to penetrate the looming fog. Seems there are many "muchs" scattered throughout a world of opportunities. Inevitably, looking back showed more than I expected at the beginning or when looking forward from each pause.

Writing has been important in my life: Writing to learn and refine ideas, writing as a way of thinking on paper, writing to connect with new information or redirect information toward new possibilities. It became a primary means to an end that seemed, well, endless.

To write a book required a beginning. Because I was not a novelist, poet, playwright, or essayist, but I enjoyed all four, I compiled them into a single volume. All deal with a touch of reality and bits of what

I learned through education, training and experience, and through continuously observing the world around me. Writing is the way I chose to act—to conclude a work that began as an idea, perhaps only a dream, and emerged from pieces scattered about like a dream shattered.

FINISHED

ACKNOWLEDGMENTS

First, my family who made life worthwhile. Second, my writing teacher and friend, Joey Madia, who engaged and encouraged me in the craft of writing and published first drafts of the *Watchman* on his website for emerging writers; and Ron Brown, Vietnam veteran and my writing classmate who listened to the first readings of drafts of much of this work and never faltered in his encouragement. Third, to Rae Jean Sielen and Andrew Rorabaugh at Populore Publishing Company for their expert guidance along the path of turning a manuscript into a book. As I am responsible for the content, errors and opinions expressed are mine alone.

ABOUT THE AUTHOR

Bill Wyant is a retired university Emeritus faculty member and research associate. His twenty-nine-year active and reserve-component Army career included branch qualifications in military intelligence and special operations.